WE ALL
FALL
DOWN

AIMEE PINARD

To Chris
For everything

Part 1:
A Love Story

Rick

The first time I saw her, she was hunched over the counter. A strand of blonde hair hung loose from her ponytail and was caught in her eyelashes. She didn't notice me walk in, didn't look up from her book when the bell chimed, notifying a customer had entered. Not being much of a reader myself, I was curious to know what book would cause someone to be so rapt. So enthralled that they couldn't pull their eyes away, even at something meant to alert you.

I don't know how long I stood there with my family's basket of dirty clothes, but when I did finally decide to move, it was because my arm was becoming sore from the weeks' worth of laundry that we'd accumulated. Usually, my mother did this sort of thing—groceries, laundromat, but last week I'd torn my meniscus at a basketball game and ended my season.

"If you're not going to play, you're going to help your mother out around here." My father had said.

So, there I was, hobbling on my throbbing knee with a crutch under my right arm, and the basket wedged against my hip in the other. The sound of dryers humming and washing machines swishing kept a strange barrier between me and the girl at the counter. There was only one other customer, but he was so deeply asleep that his mouth hung open, and an embarrassing trickle of drool slid down his slack jaw and made a stain on the collar of his shirt.

I tried to keep my back to her, to not stare at this girl with sun-bleached hair who loves to read. But having never seen her before, something in me *needed* to know who she was. I was drawn to her in a way I'd never experienced with any girl before, and being 17, that's saying something. But my mother was a feminist before feminism was a thing and taught me that not all women wanted to be approached. That most just wanted to be left the hell alone. That, coupled with my introverted nature, I resigned myself to sorting darks from lights and spending my Saturday afternoon at the laundromat instead of hanging out at my best bud, Todd's house. My mother, the feminist, did not like Todd as she claimed his father had a wandering eye and Todd would learn that same poor behavior. Behavior that served no man (or woman) any good.

There were several places to sit and wait, but I choose the one that offered me a visual of the girl. She never looked up. Her delicate finger just turned page after page, as she shifted her weight and rested her chin on her fist, sighing occasionally. The man in the back snored loudly and slumped sideways. My machine buzzed, pulling my attention back to my task. I stood and cleared my throat. The girl didn't look up. I reached into my pocket for more change, whistling as I opened the washing machine and emptied the contents into the dryer on the opposite side. I was facing her now, and from this angle I noticed just how beautiful she was, and that realization made my mother's voice even louder.

Leave her alone. She just wants to read her book without being harassed.

So, I placed my coins in the slots and turned the dials. I was not going to approach her, I truly wasn't. But the machine wouldn't turn on. I tried shimmying it, checked that the coins had dropped in properly. No luck.

Now, I must talk to the girl.

I cleared my throat again and rubbed my sweaty palms on my shorts before adjusting my crutch to avoid tripping and ruining the serendipitous moment before it began. Because that's what I'd convinced myself was happening. I was not merely a hormone-driven Neanderthal. The universe had placed me there to meet *her*. If I am perfectly honest, my want to speak to her that day had nothing to do with sex. Nothing to do with, what I would soon hear, the intoxicating sound of her laugh or the heavenly shape of her body. She was meant to be mine.

Taking one timid step at a time, attempting to look as cool and casual as a guy with a crutch can, I approached her. She still wouldn't look up and by this point, it felt like a game. Like she knew I was there and was purposely not going to look up. I reached out and placed my free hand on the counter and cleared my throat again, noticing that her book was well worn and dog-eared like it meant more to her than any old story.

"What are you reading?" I asked. My heart shot up into my throat, beads of sweat dotted my hairline despite the fan she had blowing directly at where we stood.

Her eyes slowly crept from the curled pages, up to my face. Green. Her eyes were green, but one had a small black dot on the side. As I stared at her, I realized she'd finally spoken, and I heard my mother's voice once more chastising me for gawking.

"I'm sorry. W-would you please repeat that?" I asked, my insides shriveling at the sight of her face that was twisted in either repulsion or pity. Maybe that was why I hadn't had a girlfriend yet.

"The Catcher in the Rye," she said in a southern twang with a finality that told me she wasn't really interested in talking anymore to the creep that approached her in the laundromat.

But I couldn't walk away. I couldn't let this be the end of our story.

"What's it about?" I said to the top of her head, as she had already brought her attention back to her book. My face burned as she let out a heavy sigh.

"Do you need somethin'?" She sat up straighter, placing a hand on one page of the book while the other half flopped closed.

"Your name, maybe?"

"Somethin' wrong with your machine?" She tilted her head and blinked.

"Well, yes ma'am. The machine doesn't seem to be working. But I would also love to know your name."

"That one's been broken for ages. They'll never fix it," she nodded to a jar two feet away from us. "Grab some change from there." She offered, then turned back to her book.

I thanked her and shuffled over, grabbing the appropriate amount to cover my load, and moved back to my machine. The sleeping man was now on his back, his left

arm hung at an awkward angle off the bench. His knuckles were touching the grimy tiles below.

I didn't look at her again, too embarrassed by the failed attempt at flirting. But just as I folded and stacked our clothes back into the basket and was going to make my shameful walk back toward the door, I heard her southern drawl so close that it startled me. I jumped, knocking her to the ground. Forgetting I still had a bum knee, I attempted to reach and help her up, apologizing profusely, only to collapse on top of her in the most humiliating display I'd ever been part of.

"I'm so sorry! SO, SO sorry! Are you hurt?" I asked, attempting to roll from her, my knee screaming, my stomach churning.

"No. I'm not hurt. I'm Patrice." Her voice was strained as she tried to sit up. We both inspected our tangle of limbs, then the sleeping man grunted, pulling our attention to him just as he let out a righteous fart.

We were inseparable ever since.

Rick

We talked about school, about her dreams of becoming a nurse and my dreams of being the first in my family to go to college. I wanted to become an architect. Something about the precise measurements and surety of the job was soothing. She was light and easy-going but at the same time, so driven and eager. Things not only felt possible when Patrice was around, but extraordinary. As we grew closer, she began to open up more. To explain why her goals mattered so much to her. One afternoon as we strolled along our spot at the lake, she shared with me one of the most horrifying stories I'd ever heard. It should have been a red flag. I should have paid attention, but I loved her.

I watched as her mouth moved. The words flowed from her without pause or intonation, like she was reciting a story that she was completely unfazed by.

"So, you don't speak to your parents at all? Ever?" I asked, unable to fathom not having a relationship with my own parents. I was the only child; they'd poured everything into me.

We came upon a bench overlooking the lake and sat beside one another. She'd not met my parents yet, which prompted this discussion. Patrice had dreams, big ones. I wanted my mother to see that I'd chosen someone with ambition. It felt like the right time to introduce the people that meant most to me in the world.

"The last time I saw my father..." her voice shook, she roughly fisted away the tears. I clasped her hand in mine, setting them in my lap. "Let's just say, the feeling is mutual. I don't want to see him. He doesn't want to see me."

"And your mother?" I ask softly, watching her as she stared stoically out at the water.

"The reason I don't talk to my father, is because of her. And I'd really rather not talk about that...not yet. Is that okay?" Her voice was small, unusual. I'd never heard her sound like that, like she was scared.

"Of course," I replied, but the unsettling feeling I had made a little cocoon of worry in my gut. She would later admit that she'd come home from school one day, unable to open the door to the bathroom that she and her parents shared. Her mother's body was wedged against it. Patrice peered through the small crack she forced in the door and smelled blood. Her eyes caught on the bottle of pills in her mother's open hand that lay spilled across the floor.

Her dad left her to pick up the pieces alone, and somehow, she managed to continue school while working and being in every activity she could sign up for. That was impressive by anyone's standards. She had no other family, and I knew in my heart that I had to be the one to protect her. I couldn't let this magnificent person become jaded. She wouldn't know that kind of pain again.

_____

Two weeks later, I decided to ask again for her to come to dinner and meet my parents. My mother had taken to silently pacing the floor every time I left the house to spend time with Patrice, which in the three months since our fateful meeting at the laundromat had been almost every evening after I completed my chores, assignments for school, and repeated discussions about fornicating and its hellish sinfulness. My mother was a feminist, but she also did not want grandchildren out of holy wedlock. I promised my parents that I was being a complete gentleman. But mother insisted she had no way of knowing what I was truly up to, because she had not met the mystery girl who had stolen my heart.

What she really meant, was that Patrice had stolen her son. Her only child. The golden boy who was going to college the following year.

"I promise, you'll love them!" I pleaded with Patrice as we walked hand-in-hand down the sidewalk that stretched the mile from her trailer to the quaint subdivision that my home was in.

"Yeah, but will *they* love *me*?" she mused, swinging our arms back and forth between us. The cool air made her nose and cheeks blush rosy, pink.

I squeezed her hand, her fingertips icy between mine. "They have no reason not to love you." I brought her hand up and pressed a kiss against her knuckles.

"I don't do well with parents." That same cold voice from when she spoke of her mom and dad made that cocoon in my gut shimmy.

"You will with mine. What about Wednesday evening?" I refused to let her fears overtake her opportunity. She had too much to offer, too much to look forward to than to shy away from a family who would love her.

"I'm going to Ronni's to study on Wednesday after I get off my shift."

"Why don't you come study with me?"

"Because I'm always with you! I kind of miss my girl time," she teased, shoving her shoulder into mine.

I admit, I did love having Patrice all to myself. I couldn't play ball anymore, and my buddies were all preparing for tournaments and making sure scouts would see them. I had my own studies, and I had Patrice.

"What about Thursday?" I smiled because she was hardheaded and liked making me work for things. "You don't work Thursday, and you'll have taken your test."

She stopped, abruptly facing me, her dazzling eyes boring into mine. "You're not going to give up, are you?" A breeze blew her hair into her face. She'd been wearing it down lately. I loved it that way.

"Nope!" I hugged her to me and relaxed as I felt her arms wrap around my waist.

"Ok. But if they hate me, you only have yourself to blame," she mumbled into my chest.

"No one could ever hate you," I sighed with the relief that I'd won without having to go through the entire bulleted list of reasons why she should trust me with this. I didn't want to force her, but it was feeling more and more that we were only a couple around her schedule, her social life. I'd only met her friends in passing, and having no family of her own, I needed things between us to feel more solid and committed.

"On the contrary, dear boy," she whirled around, tapped a finger to her chin, and shivered as another breeze blew through. The cicadas rattled in the bushes as the sun began to make its slow descent along the horizon. "If your mother hates you enough to kill herself, one can assume that the possibility of being hated by others is very strong."

Rick

I'd offered to pick her up, so she didn't feel intimidated walking up to my house alone. But Patrice wasn't a woman who needed a security blanket. My father gave an approving nod over his crossword puzzle when I said as much. Mother wrung her hands and mumbled something as she disappeared into the hallway to vacuum the already spotless carpet.

"She's just nervous," my father said to me in that comforting tone he used when my mother found herself fussing over things that were out of her control. "You've never brought a girl home before."

"That's because no other girl is like Patrice." I looked out the window that faced the street, waiting to see her turn the corner.

"Felt the same way about your mother," he said in a way that made me turn back to face him, because in that moment it all came together for me. Patrice was not like any other girl, and I didn't need to date anyone else to confirm what I already knew.

"I think she might be the *one*, Dad."

I heard my mother slam a cabinet in whatever room she was eavesdropping from. My father casually placed his crossword in his lap and folded his hands on top of it before looking me in the eye.

"Well then son, I can't wait to meet her."

The sound of our doorbell pulled my gaze back to the window where I could see her standing confidently at the front door to my right. She fidgeted with her hair and smoothed her skirt. She wore a dark pea-coat over a green dress that I'd not seen on her before, and I was touched to think she'd gone through the effort of purchasing something new for the occasion. Her hair spilled in loose curls over her shoulders with a piece at the top pinned to the side to accentuate her heart-shaped face.

"Are you going to get the door or just make her wait until the postman comes?" My mother spoke from behind me.

"Oh...right," I replied and took three clipped steps to the door.

"Patrice! So very lovely to finally meet you!" Mother said over my shoulder. I was a bit taken aback by the look on Patrice's face. She didn't appear as self-assured from this angle as she had from my view at the window.

"Hello, Mrs. Adams," Patrice spoke carefully, as though my mother was standing beside me with a butcher knife.

"Won't you come in!" My father came up on my right side and placed a firm hand on my shoulder, grinning widely at Patrice. My mother complimented her dress as she helped to remove her coat and hung it on the coat rack beside the door.

Patrice didn't reply, rather timidly stepped inside with a tight smile on her lips. I escorted her to the dinner table that my mother spent much too long setting, adjusting, removing, and replacing bits of things to make it just right.

My father thanked my mother for her efforts, kissing her lightly on the cheek as he does so often that it's not remarkable to me, but Patrice's eyes grew wide, her face flushed.

"I told you, they're harmless," I teased, giving Patrice a wink as she picked at her fingernails in her lap.

"I don't know that I can do this," she whispered out of the corner of her mouth. My heart plummeted.

"Do what? Have dinner? Do you feel ill?" I asked, thinking it was the only reasonable explanation why she would be acting so peculiar.

"I told you. I don't do parents," she swallowed, her face paled to a color that matched mother's hand-stitched seat covers.

I reached over and tried to hold her hand, give her some reassurance and was even more surprised to find she was trembling. My mother whisked over to us with a beautiful roast and placed it at the center of the table. My father held a pitcher of water and made a ceremony of pouring it into each of our glasses.

"Th-thank you, Sir." Patrice cleared her throat.

"Call me, Jeff. From what I understand, you two are quite serious. No Mr. Adams or Sir around here when we are amongst family."

Patrice let out a cough, and heat burned the back of my neck and tips of my ears. She didn't know that he spoke to everyone like this. My father didn't know a stranger. He considered the bagger at the grocery store family and knew everything about him from his mother's ingrown toenail to the three-legged dog they rescued.

"Oh, Jeff. Don't embarrass them. You're going to scare her off before she even gets to know us properly!" My mother gave him a playful slap on the arm, and they embraced again which made Patrice's leg begin to bounce wildly under the table.

This was their way. An endearing teeter-totter of having spent the majority of their lives together. When one dropped off, the other picked up. There was something in my mother's eyes, however, that I couldn't quite interpret.

"Patrice is planning to go to nursing school once she graduates. Isn't that something?" I announce, hoping to rid the room of whatever awkward tension was brewing.

"Nursing! Wow, how about that, June?" My father turned to my mother, genuinely pleased.

"That's wonderful, dear! What made you decide that?" she asked, leaning forward, and stabbing at a slice of roast to place onto Patrice's plate. Seconds of silence passed while my mom continued to scoop rice and green beans from my father's helpful hands.

Patrice stared at the lump of rice and steaming meat on her plate. We all watched her, waiting for the story to come as she licked her lips, sorting her thoughts.

"I've just always had an interest in it. In knowing how to fix things...on the body," she said, her words cautiously constructed to form the sentence that my parents would deem fit.

"How interesting. I wish I had a passion like that at your age. Now, I'm just a homemaker. But I can sew a button in 30-seconds flat!" My mother jabbed her finger into the air with pride. She never complained about being home. In truth, I had no idea what my mother's interests outside of me and my father were. Or if she had any at all.

"Oh, dear. You are so much more than a homemaker," my father crooned, leaning over to give her a gentle nudge.

I removed my hand from Patrice's so that I could serve myself. I ignored the dampness on my palms, but she wiped hers down her skirt before reaching for her fork.

"Yes." Patrice replied, her face blank.

"I bet your parents must be so proud of you!" My mother added, and it's as if time stopped. Like the floor was falling out beneath us, but their faces were frozen in those unknowing, ignorant smiles. The sound of Patrice's chair clattering against the floor jolted me back into reality.

"I'm so very sorry. I just, I just don't fit here." She hopped over the legs of the chair, stumbling toward the door, forgetting her coat.

"Was it something I said?" Mother whispered.

I chased after Patrice, tugging her coat off the rack on my way out.

"I'm so sorry. I didn't tell them about your parents. I didn't feel it was my place!" I called out to her as she reached the corner to turn left back toward her trailer.

"That's just it, Rick. That's what you don't get. I'm not ever going to be the girl you're proud to have on your arm. Especially not with parents like that."

"You don't like my parents?"

"No! Your parents are lovely, and your home smells of home cooking and there's no cigarette burns in your carpet or dead shrubs in your flowerbed. Once the newness of us wears off, you'll see that and prefer someone else.

Someone with a decent pedigree and who doesn't feel like bolting when she sees parents kiss because she fears it's only a precursor to a fight."

I shift my weight from one foot to the other, digesting her worries. She doesn't walk away so I take slow, steady steps toward her. "So, let's make our own story. Me and you. We don't have to be like your parents, and we don't have to be like my parents. We can be *us*." I wrap the coat around her, pulling it closed at her waist as she shivered violently from nerves and the cold.

"And what if we turn out like mine?" She asked, her eyes welled with tears.

"What if we don't," I counter, leaning forward, my eyes on those full, beautiful lips before she met me halfway.

Nothing else mattered in that moment. I knew everything I needed to know. We were going to make this work. We would support one another, and I would make her feel safe and loved. No pressure in being perfect, no expectations. I could do that for her.

I wanted desperately to do that for her.

Rick

"Oklahoma is playing at the cinema. We should go!" I slid up next to Patrice just as she shoved a few books in her locker. Since meeting my parents, we'd decided family dinners were not necessary. My mother remained surprisingly silent about my relationship with Patrice, and my father only asked that before I made any permanent decisions, to truly think it through. Being a person who spends most of his days thinking only of his future, I assured him that I was keeping a level head. Patrice had limits. I would learn how to navigate them the same way she would offer the same in return for me.

As we grew closer, I learned her schedule and enjoyed walking her to class. I took a bit of pride in watching her friends' envious stares when they'd see roses on her seat as she walked through the classroom door. It felt good knowing guys wished she was with them, but she was *mine*. I made sure she never had a reason to look at anyone else, because I knew nobody could ever make her feel as happy and treasured as I would.

Together, we could do anything and that made me hopeful for our future. The closer I came to graduation, the more I didn't feel like having friends in high school was all that important. If you thought about it, you'll never see those people again because most who grew up here, couldn't wait to get the hell out. I didn't want Patrice to fall into the footsteps of her parents and end up having regrets. She was too special and had too much to offer the world than to waste it on anything that would steer her off track. I looked forward to the day when I would walk across that stage and know with certainty what lay ahead for us.

"Sure." She didn't look up at me, rather just stared into the shadows of her locker. "A movie sounds great."

"Something wrong?" I asked, offering to carry her books as she softly closed her locker door, pressing it gently until it latched shut.

"The girls got together this weekend and didn't invite me," she furrowed her brow, looking up at me in pained confusion. I know it hurt her feelings when her friends didn't include her as much anymore, or sit with us at the prom, but it just further proved my point that they didn't really care about her the way I did.

"I'm sorry. Who needs them anyway?" I gave her a light jab and turned toward her classroom.

"Well I do, Rick," she stopped walking and tilted her head. "You graduate in a month. I'll be here for another year. I need friends. I *want* friends."

I paused, realizing what a jerk I'd been. One of my old buddies from basketball elbowed me and waved as he walked by, hand-in-hand with his girl who was in deep discussion with the girl on her right. Looking over Patrice's shoulder, I noticed most everyone seemed to have relationships outside of their significant other.

"I've been selfish and sucked up all of your free time, haven't I?" I raised my eyebrows and smiled, hoping she would forgive me for unknowingly driving a wedge in her friendships.

"Maybe a little bit." She held up her fingers showing me the inch-sized wedge of Rick.

"Look. I'll buy tickets for you and your friends. You go to the movie. We can celebrate our one-year later," I winked and continued walking past her.

I see her slap her palm to her forehead in my peripheral.

"Oh, Rick! I'm an idiot! Our anniversary is Friday, isn't it?" She rushed up beside me. A teacher grumbled about class needing to begin, and that we'd better move along.

"No, no. We still have the rest of the weekend. I'll just have to make *our* date extra special." I kiss her on the tip of her nose and tuck a strand of hair behind her ear.

"Really? You don't mind?" she asked, grinning ear-to-ear as she shuffled toward her classroom.

"We have forever. They can have Friday night," I say, because what I have planned is far more important than the movie.

Reflecting on the past always gives you more perspective, hindsight being 20/20 and all. At the time, I couldn't see beyond how deeply I loved her, how drawn I was to her ambitions. Looking back as an adult man, I was able to understand that my parents had their own reservations but wanted me to figure it out for myself and make my own decisions. I admit, if they'd have tried to get me to split up with Patrice, I would have never spoken to them again. Hell, I'd barely spoken to my own friends who tried as much.

So, as I stood waiting for her friends to bring her in secret after the movie. I'd asked that they drive her to our spot overlooking the lake at the municipal pier. I ignored the nagging little voice telling me to run the other way. I'd increasingly found myself explaining away her oddities, like when she would claim she'd forgotten to eat or that she wasn't hungry at all for days, or her mood swings which I chalked up to her time of the month. I wasn't a man who was turned off by such things, my mother taught me about a woman's body outside of what most men were interested in.

I simply accepted all of her. I lit candles in the shape of a heart. Her friends were instructed to blind fold her so when she opened her eyes, the first thing she'd see was me on one knee. She looked so beautiful that night, standing there with the wind whipping her hair and dress, her eyes glistening behind her tears in the moonlight as she took in the scene. Her friends squealed behind her, hopping up and down at how romantic it was.

Patrice was wearing a white summer dress that kissed the tops of her bare feet. I paused a moment wondering where her shoes were and if she'd gone to the theater without them. The candles below cast dancing shadows on her face and lit her up as if she were an angel from Heaven. The sound of cicadas always a part of my memories with her. Our own personal chorus. I will remember that night for the rest of my life. Her friends slowly stepped back, their feet shuffling in the soft, wet grass. My left knee now soaked through, but I didn't care. I would have stayed that way forever if it meant she'd always look exactly as she did right then.

"Patrice Nadine Carter, I have loved you since the very moment I saw you. In the last year, you've taught me so much about life and opened my eyes in ways that have made me a better man. I know I have so much more to learn, and I am sure to be a bonehead from time to time, but if you can see past that, I promise that I'll try to be better for you, for the rest of your life. Will you marry me?"

I heard her friends scream with glee as Patrice clamped her hands over her mouth. Her entire body trembled as she let out a sob. I mentally pushed aside something in the split second after she choked out "Yes!". Something I hadn't allowed myself to focus on at the time, but over the years has haunted me. I ignored it, because I loved her more than whatever it was trying to warn me from. I was confident we could overcome any obstacle. Despite what we went through, and despite what she continued to do, I stayed. Because even as her worst, even after what she did to us...I loved her.

Rick

Married life was not quit what I expected. After an intimate celebration with close friends and my parents, I rented a modest apartment close to the community college where I was taking some prerequisites until Patrice graduated high school. We sold her trailer and used that money to buy a car and some furniture for our home. My mother froze several casseroles for us to have while Patrice and I maintained our busy schedules.

"And how are things?" Mother always asked when she made her weekly calls to check in.

"Things are great! We are working hard, Patrice is graduating early so she will start her classes at the community college soon while we save up for nursing school," I lied.

In the months since our nuptials, Patrice seemed to grow less and less interested in the things that used to light her fire. I knew if I told my mother, she would offer unbiased, sage advice. But I didn't want to have to admit I might have rushed things. I thought I'd known everything I needed to know in order to be the perfect husband for her. I hadn't had the foresight to see that I, too, would have needs one day. She never seemed to consider me either.

I had a rare, free evening the Thursday before Patrice's 19th birthday, so I checked her schedule and was pleased to find that her shift at the laundromat was over by 6:00pm. I made reservations at her favorite Italian place, laid out a dress and shoes for her to change into and quickly tidied our mess of an apartment. Bearing in mind her job, I'd assumed she would take on—at least—that role as I did most everything else, but as I took inventory in the two hours I'd spent scrubbing counters and finding underwear in places no one should be leaving their unmentionables, I realized we needed to discuss the division of household duties.

"Well, that's very chauvinistic of you to assume I'd be doing the laundry," she said, crossing her arms over her sweater that had a week-old spaghetti stain.

"You *work* at the *laundromat*, Patrice!" I paced the 10-feet of the living area, gesticulating. "We met when I was doing my family's laundry! I'm not assuming you'll do it because you're a woman. I'm assuming you'll do it because you *work there!*" I had never raised my voice at Patrice, not ever. But I was quite frustrated having come from some major exams into an apartment that smelled of rotten food and mildewed towels.

"Well, I'm sorry I'm not Little Miss Susie Homemaker like your mother!" She slumped back on the sofa, ripping her sweater off.

"Don't be ugly about my mother. She's been nothing but kind to you!"

"Right. All the times she's visited, she's been lovely," Patrice rolled her eyes. My parents have not been over since we moved in 6 months ago.

"I haven't invited them in hopes you would," I clenched my teeth, working very hard to remain calm.

"I told you—"

"Don't even say it! I'll shit if you say that silly thing about parents once more time, Patrice!" I clutched at my hair, fisting it and sucking air in controlled counts.

"Ugh! What do you want from me?!" She flung her arms in the air.

"I want you to be the woman I fell in love with! Sometimes, I don't even feel like you love me at all!"

"Well, soooorry I'm not perfect!" At that, she burst into tears and curled into the fetal position. Her tears trickled down her cheeks and onto the sofa cushion.

"Oh, don't give me that. You don't get to play victim! I've done everything for you!" I tripped over a shoe and kicked it across the floor, watching it thud against a blackened banana peel that had just missed the trashcan. "This place is a pigsty!"

"Victim?! You *sold* my *home*!" She slapped at her chest, her words coming out in violent huffs.

"Home?! *This* is our home! Not that godawful roach box!"

At that, she chucked the TV remote at me. It clipped my ear and crashed into the wall behind me, shattering to the floor. She stared as the batteries that rolled at my feet.

Things went on like that for hours. Her blaming me for the immense sadness that befell her, and me maddeningly trying to convince her that everything I'd done was only for her happiness, for *our* happiness. We missed our dinner reservations.

When we finally ran out of reasons to blame one another for the disaster than had become our relationship, I blew out a long breath and went over to where she

26

remained a tight ball of despair, placed a hand on her back and began rubbing in circles to calm her. "I don't want you to be perfect. I just want to understand what changed between us?"

"I don't know!" She sobbed, snot dripping from her red nose. She wiped at it with the back of her hand, her red-rimmed eyes making the green pop even more. "I just don't feel like myself anymore. I can't explain it, but I don't know what I want like I used to. I have no purpose, and now I feel like you're being forced to treat me like a child."

I had been noticing her emotional decline for some time. I convinced myself it would resolve, eventually. A strange season most people deal with at one point or another. We had moved quickly. Her world was different now as a wife, even if not many obvious things had changed. Her friends were not wives, they had certain freedoms that married couples did not, bills they didn't need to worry about yet, obligations they did not have to meet.

Patrice had a point. Everything we originally discussed, was not happening. But when I tried to discuss our future, she would brush it off with one of her incredible smiles and say that those things would come naturally and not to force it. Standing in our living room that day, I saw that I failed to take charge. She needed a reason to push through the harder moments *because* she was a wife. Patrice always needed stability.

I leaned in and lightly kissed her swollen lips, a wave of want crept down my body, making me swell against my jeans.

"It's been a while since we..." she whispered against my lips making me dizzy. Patrice had that way about her.

One minute she was a ball of wild fury and the next, a sultry wife who hungered for her husband.

"Yes... it has," I slowly kissed her again, groaning as she matched my desire. Our bodies came together like they hadn't before, even since our first time making love the night we were married. Patrice needed purpose. So that evening, I decided not to wear a condom and she was too caught up in our passion to notice. I knew she would be a wonderful mother, but our small apartment would not be sufficient for a family. We would need space. I decided to make my own sacrifice and drop-out of school.

When eight-weeks passed and she finally noticed her cycle had not come, she had me drive her to the doctor to confirm what I already knew. She wanted to see the doctor alone, so I sat patiently in the waiting room, watching the clock tick by until she emerged from the narrow hallway half an hour later.

"I'm pregnant," she said with no real recognizable tone.

I clapped and shot out of my seat, grabbing her and spinning us in a circle as I whooped and rejoiced in our fertility.

"A baby! Oh, Patrice we are going to be parents! I can't believe it!" I wasn't surprised that I'd begun to tear up. I always knew we would become a family, but to have it confirmed was altogether different. Another odd feeling, however, was how stiff her body felt in my arms. She had not returned my embrace. She was not sharing my tears of unbridled joy.

I gently set her down, suddenly aware of the life we'd created that I was meant to protect. "I'm so sorry. I was just overcome!" I breathed out, kissing her dry lips as she remained still. "What is it?" I asked.

"I told you. I don't do parents," she said, her face frozen with what I understood immediately, was a quiet rage. The woman behind the counter shrank in her seat, trying to appear busy despite the deafening silence before I replied.

"We will make our own story, remember? We get to decide what kind of parents our baby will have!" I gripped her shoulders, trying to make eye contact with her so she could see in my eyes how strongly I believed in us.

"No, Rick. *You* decided," she gritted her teeth and pulled away from me. I flushed with embarrassment as the woman at the counter tried looking anywhere else, but I did have to pay for the visit. There was no escaping this awkward situation. I made my way to the counter as Patrice yanked the door open and marched out.

I tucked my tail and found Patrice in the parking lot, leaning against my car. We did not speak on the way home. I did not get to surprise her with the photo of our new home that I had tucked in my back pocket. One that was across from another young couple that we would have dinners with and hopefully, raise children with. It was a crisp, white-bricked single-story with a forest green front door and surrounded by trees. I'd looked at so many, waiting for one to speak to me, to tell me it was where I should raise my family. The moment I stood in front of that one, I knew right away. I'd fumbled for my camera and snapped the photo.

I also did not get to tell her that I'd taken a job at an insurance agency that offered a decent salary, plus commission. That was all fine. She needed time to process. That was her way. Soon, she would understand and become excited with a renewed zest for life. She would bring home baby clothes and sing those cute little nursery rhymes to her belly. She was going to be so happy. I made a good decision, and I knew it would make everything better. Everything was going to be just fine.

AIMEE PINARD

Becky

That woman had a few screws loose. More than a few, but Ted encouraged me to welcome her since she didn't seem to have many friends. Or friends at all. I had heard rumblings about her around town. Patrice's family wasn't known for being upstanding members of the community. My mother heard from her friend that Patrice's mother was a whack-job and offed herself right in front of the child. She also heard that Patrice's father was philandering about, not even trying to hide it. Apparently, the apple didn't fall too far from the tree.

"I have no idea how she roped her husband into marrying her, but the word is she got knocked up and he did the *honorable thing*"," Marie sipped her tea, then placed it gently on the doily I slid in front of her, waiting for her to compliment it. I'd spent hours working on that particular one.

"She's never worked a day in her life, I bet. At the first opportunity to marry up, she took it," Teresa added. Marie and Teresa were older than me. Their children were starting high school in the fall, so their time was mainly spent eavesdropping and gossiping. I poured myself a cup and carefully placed it on my own doily that was not quite as well done as theirs. That year, I'd taken up many hobbies. I'd actually befriended Marie in a knitting group. Teresa taught

31

me how to keep my flowerbeds lush year-round, and in the recent weeks before Patrice consumed all conversations, I'd taught myself how to make doilies. It's what women did when they didn't have children and needed to prove they were not at all bothered by the empty nursery. I wouldn't need these meaningless distractions anymore, though. But, I wanted Ted to be the first to know. As I stared blankly at the center of the table where the plate of cucumber sandwiches sat untouched. I was startled by the silence that fell. I blinked and looked up at their expectant faces, waiting for me to add in my remarks on the strange couple who moved in across the street.

"The woman can't even prepare toast. All she does is aimlessly walk around like she has nothing else to do. Sometimes, though there will be hours she just disappears. I never see anyone visit their house. Not a mother, friend, neighbor. Just me and Ted. The husband seems nice enough," I sipped, placed my cup down and made a show of pouring them each another cup, repositioning them until finally Marie gasped.

"Becky, these doilies are fantastic! Did you make them yourself?" She ran her fingers over the scalloped edges as Teresa *oohed* and *ahhed* along with her.

I sat up proudly, "I did."

—

After the ladies left, I stared out of my bay window, my own hand pressed to my not-yet bump. The oak tree in the center of our yard partially blocked my view, but it also allowed me the opportunity to spy on the neighbors without being considered nosey. Marie's words played over and over in my head about the very young, very pretty Patrice being pregnant and trapping that poor man. If she was, she'd not been far enough along to show it, but since Marie put the thought in my mind, I did notice the way she placed a hand protectively over her belly as she paced the sidewalk. I wondered if she had her nursery set up yet. It didn't seem like she did anything other than that creepy pacing up and down, in and out.

"You should go talk to her," Ted encouraged for probably the fourth time in two weeks. He'd just come in from work, his jacket wafted the scent of cigar smoke as he hung it on the rack beside me. Ted was always more social than I was. "You're both young, and I bet she would love learning about any of your hobbies!"

"My hobbies are temporary," I ran my fingers down the sheer curtain. "I won't have much time for them when we have a baby."

"Right," he said, turning me around and pressing a firm kiss to my lips. "I just mean that it would be good for you to make friends with someone more your age. Marie and Teresa are nice, but you don't have much in common with them," he pulled off his shoes, set them in the closet by the door and walked into the nook he'd built into a bar. I watched as he poured himself a scotch. He stopped asking about my barren womb months ago, which will make today's news all the more exciting.

"I don't think I'll have much in common with *her* either," I crossed my arms in front of me. "She doesn't seem to be the kind of woman I should be close with."

"Oh, Becks," Ted tilted his head and smiled. He hadn't used that nickname in so long. That empty room weighed as heavily on his heart as it did on mine. "You never know how much you need a friend, until you have one. Sure, she may be a little odd, but maybe *she* really needs a friend."

I sighed. Ted was right, as he often was with his pearls of wisdom and surplus of kindness. "You're right. I'll walk over next time she's out. Maybe we can shop for baby clothes together..." I let the words hang in the air, watching his expression shift from casual acknowledgment to the understanding of what I've just admitted. We made love three times that night.

Rick

I couldn't help but feel validated when I noticed her beginning to embrace the pregnancy. She started to slowly bring baby clothes home, all delicate lace and soft pinks in hopes that we would have a girl. All I wanted was a healthy baby, a bridge to mend the ever-growing gap between my parents and our life. Patrice danced around to Elvis crooning through the record player with her hand delicately pressed to her rounded belly. I was euphoric, because finally we felt like a real family. We even started having card night with the neighbors Becky and Ted Leonard who were expecting as well. Things could not have been falling into place more smoothly.

Becky had been such a blessing for Patrice. When we first moved in, I could see that my wife was not adjusting as quickly as I had hoped she would. I'd often come home after a long day's work and find her aimlessly walking the neighborhood. I'd bought her books, but she didn't like reading much. I encouraged her to meet the neighbors, and she would reply with that same listless wave of her hand that she'd use in place of words.

But one day, I noticed a pie on the counter.

"Oh! Honey, did you bake this?! It looks amazing!" I dropped my briefcase on the kitchen table and rushed for a fork and plate.

"Becky brought it over earlier. She's nice."

Those seven words were like music to my ears. My wife had made a friend. "Lovely, that's just lovely! Maybe we can have them over for dinner this weekend. I'll cook! Why don't you see if they're free?"

"Sure, dear. I'll do that." She smiled and lowered into the rocker my mother sent over last week. It had been the one she rocked me in as a baby. I teared up at the sentiment, brushing away the hurt that she hadn't brought it herself.

In the following months, Patrice blossomed. She began to decorate our home when she wasn't in school and bought herself a cook book, testing a new recipe every night. The light in her eyes shone brighter and it all felt like what we'd dreamed our life to look like from when we first met.

I still remember when I got the call that our baby was on the way. I couldn't contain my excitement. I hurriedly excused myself from work, bumping into every person on my way out, pouring apologies as I rushed toward my car. I tried to keep her calm and breathing on the way to the hospital just like we'd read about. Fifteen minutes later, we arrived at the hospital and thirty after that, I was pacing the waiting room. I could hear her cries and itched to be by her side, holding her hand, reminding her to do the breathing exercises. *In through the nose, out through the mouth, Patrice.* I had been offered a coffee, soda, water, chips, a seat, but who could think of anything else at a time like this? I had to be ready for the moment our baby arrived! I did a quick run to the gift shop and browsed baby gifts. What would be the perfect way to say, *Thank you for having my baby!?* I settled on a large pink bouquet. She had been convinced the entire time that we were having a girl. I guess it was that motherly instinct you always hear about.

An hour later, the doctor came out with a huge grin, congratulating me and ushered me back to where Patrice was recovering. I knew distinctly in that moment that something shifted. It wasn't what you would think the room to be like once a woman sees her cooing child for the first time. The air felt dense as I stepped through the door. Patrice was lying there, staring out the window, watching birds fluttering around.

"So, my love, how are you feeling? Do you need anything? I brought you some flowers!" I beamed. "I wanted to see you before I go down to the nursery." She continued to stare out the window a few more moments, and then slowly turned her head to me.

"What am I supposed to do with a boy, Rick." She said it like a statement, like she wasn't actually waiting on a response from me. Her words shot straight into my chest like a dagger. The color had left her face, and her hair was matted with sweat. The doctor said that it was normal to be emotional after having had a long labor, and she would improve over time. I tried to swallow back my disappointment. I had failed her. But, I knew I would make things right. I knew she was exhausted.

Once we arrived home, Becky and Ted brought over some lasagna and pie for us. I was so thankful that she and Patrice had hit it off. She needed a friend's support now more than ever. One that she would be able to confide it since it clearly wasn't me. Nevertheless, I noticed my wife slowly getting back to normal. After a few weeks, she seemed to warm up to John just as the doctor assured, she would. She took to motherhood like a duck to water. Well, maybe more like a baby deer taking its first steps, but she was great. My wife was glowing and watching her with John made me fall even more in love with her.

However, she had taken to sleeping in the spare bedroom so that John wouldn't wake her. I was happy to have those early moments with him and understood how exhausting have an infant could be. She'd come back. Only as the months passed, she remained in the room and the longer she stayed, the more painful it was to talk about. Eventually, I moved John to the room across the hall from her, and I would now and again catch him crawling outside her door, listening to her sing along to her records, or watching her delicately putting her makeup on. He adored her as much as I did.

I bet she didn't even realize how much happier she would be with a child of her own. But what I couldn't admit to myself, the reason I didn't demand her to come back to our room, was because when Becky had not yet given birth, they spent all of their time together, preparing casseroles to stick in the freezer. Patrice helped to knit booties and stocked their baby room full of essentials. Becky helped with John during the day, and I never anticipated her giving birth would become such a devastating event. Because while Patrice had to accept that I'd given her a boy, she couldn't get past the jealousy of her best friend giving birth to a happy, healthy baby girl.

Becky

"He really is a darling boy, Patrice," I cooed over John, his small fist curled around the dinosaur figurine I'd bought him for his first birthday. I was smitten by the little prince and even with my sweet little Eve, there was something so special about his precious smile and big brown eyes. Part of me wondered if I loved him so much because Patrice...well...she didn't. In the beginning, she seemed to make more of an effort but as the months went by, she became more and more detached. It was so odd and inappropriate to me to see her want to spend more time hovering over Eve than making sure he had a clean diaper. Or that he was fed.

John was such a good little baby too and clearly adored his mother. It was a shame how she would act as though he was pestering her, like his needs were a major inconvenience. Some days she seemed to try harder than others but something was off, and it made me quite uncomfortable. I definitely didn't want to invite her to my tea dates with the girls. What if she acted strangely in front of them? What would they think of me?

"Do you ever wonder what it would be like if you'd married someone else?" she mused, folding a load of clothes while I fed the children.

"What do you mean?" I knew exactly what she meant. The rumors had been circulating for a while now, but it was not my place to ask. In fact, I didn't really want her to talk to me about it at all.

"Like do you ever feel bored in your life with Ted? Crave someone more exciting, fun, better sex?" The corner of her mouth twitched up into a smirk that made me fight my own instinct to make the sign of the cross.

"Never!" I gasped. "I love Ted. I love our life." I was only partially lying. "Why? Are you unhappy with Rick?"

She stayed quiet, a dramatic stretch of silence between us as she contemplated whether or not to further this particular discussion. Crossing such a boundary was risky, a test to any friendship. Marie and Teresa had already tried getting any juicy bits from me when we've had our weekly tea sessions, but mums the word. I had become intrigued by Patrice and her husband who worshipped the ground she walked on, or danced on, or left piles of dirty clothes and dishes for weeks on end for one stretch of time, while cleaning with maddening focus for another.

"No. Not unhappy. Just bored," she shrugged as though it were entirely natural indeed to consider hopping into another man's bed citing boredom.

"So...have you?" I eyed her while keeping my expression neutral, non-judgmental. Friendly.

I'll never forget the look on her face as she turned toward me, dropping the onesie she was holding. Her cheeky smile as she arched an eyebrow. "I can't tell you all my secrets, Becky."

A slight chill ran down my spine as she hinted at being an adulteress. I am a Christian woman and it took a considerable amount of effort to befriend such a woman as Patrice. Especially after what happened at the supermarket. Boy, was that a doozy.

I wasn't there, but Teresa was picking up some mixers for her monthly Bingo night and saw the *whole* thing. Apparently, John wanted a sucker and started to cry. Instead of getting the poor boy the damn sucker, she went ballistic. As if *she* was the child. She screamed and stomped her feet and spit and threw herself on the ground...I mean it was quite the scene. Teresa said it took two security guards and the store manager to restrain her.

At the end of it, she looked like a mental case. Drenched in sweat, snot running down into her mouth. How embarrassing for Rick. And what makes the whole thing even more strange, is she kept trying to blame John! Apparently, that event forced Rick into hiring a "nanny" which we all understood was basically a babysitter for Patrice. Nobody wanted to be around her after that, and her mood swings occurred more frequently. I swear when I'd be trying to tell her a story, she would zone out completely. I tested her one time and told her that my mother was from Mobile, but she's actually from Montgomery and later I told her how we were supposed to go visit my mother in Montgomery, and she didn't even question it!

So, with her little non-confession, I decided not to divulge to the other ladies. For whatever reason, it felt like something I wanted to keep in my own back pocket, in case. In case of what? I couldn't tell you, but I had a full view of the rollercoaster ride that was Patrice Adams, and that woman really is odd. Don't even get me started on the time she almost killed the boy.

Rick

Things didn't take a turn for the worse right away. As the days went on, pieces of her vanished bit by excruciating bit. I began to miss it, miss her and the life we could have had together. I thought that maybe it was a family she desired, but struggled with balancing the idea of a having a child while going to school. I assured her that she could handle anything, but it became abundantly clear that I was profoundly wrong.

My phone trilled on my desk in the office I'd been moved to. I started in a cubicle when I initially landed this job. My parent's protests rang in my ears for months, making me wonder if I'd made a mistake dropping out of school. My pod mate was a man who smelled of cat piss and rarely wore pants that properly zipped. All those combined were incentive enough to hit numbers so my boss would look to me first for the promotion. Which he did.

"Rick Adams speaking!" I sang proudly into the receiver.

"Heya, Rick. It's Bob." He sounded disappointed saying his own name. I'd grown up with him, we'd learned to ride bikes together and snuck into his father's liquor cabinet once when we were kids. He was a good man, a friend, and hearing him sound this way was unusual.

"Everything alright?" I ask, moving my phone from one shoulder to the other.

"It's Patrice. She had a bit of a...an *episode* in the middle of the store. I hate calling you up at work, but I can't get her to calm down." As he spoke, it sounded like he was covering his mouth as not to be overheard.

My face burned with humiliation. Patrice had anxiety attacks before, but not to this extent. Not in public.

"I'll be there in ten minutes," I said, offering my apologies before hanging up and alerting my boss that I would return as soon as I could. I rushed over, hardly coming to complete stops at every stop sign. I found her, surrounded by dozens of people who were not helping, just watching on in horror. They were all stunned by the charade my wife was putting on for all to see, not even realizing how quickly word would spread about this, irreparably scarring the Adams' name.

John was sitting in the shopping cart, staring down at her. He was wearing only one shoe and a t-shirt stained with what seems to have been a red sucker. I helped Patrice off of the floor and into the car, her body clung to me like I was a life raft. She was shivering despite it being unseasonably warm out. I couldn't look Bob in the eye, or anyone else for that matter.

I drove them home—confirming that Patrice would be okay for the few hours until I could return—and went back to work, sweat dripping down my back, heart racing but it had only been about forty minutes. I assured my boss I would not be taking a lunch to make up for the time lost. I spent the rest of the afternoon toggling between how to help my wife and how to keep my job. Her outbursts were becoming harder and harder to keep private, and although my mother offered dozens of times to come help with John, I knew it would only anger Patrice more.

Living in a small town was a blessing and a curse. I was grateful to Bob for calling me instead of the police. I was thankful that Becky was so loving of John. By the end of the workday, I didn't feel as shaken. No marriage is perfect, but I made a vow to Patrice and she deserved my support now more than ever. With a renewed sense of calm, I walked to my car, rubbing my arms against the chill in the air. It had been so hot earlier in contrast, but the cool front had changed temperature abruptly, the mark of seasons changing and holidays approaching. Once in my car, I turned up the radio.

Flash flood warning in effect.... The DJ droned under the clap of thunder. Rain clouds hovered, squeezing out a downpour just as I pulled out of the parking lot. I whistled along to the music and looked forward to curling up with John on the couch after dinner. However, the closer I got to our street, the more uneasy I felt. Something was wrong.

The first thing I saw when I turned the corner was Becky, frantically rushing from her house to mine. I squinted against the downpour, brought my speed to a crawl and parallel parked beside my driveway. I should have been in more of a hurry, but my limbs felt heavy as though weighted with sacks of sand. Opening my car door, I stepped out and my foot sloshed in a stream of rushing water that pooled at the edge of the curb. I swung my other leg and hopped up onto the sidewalk, sprinting up my driveway where I crashed into Becky who was sobbing, her hands shaking as she grabs tightly onto my shoulders.

"I didn't call the police," she sputtered, her nails digging into my skin through my shirt.

"What happened? Is it Patrice? John?" Bile rose up my throat. I pushed past her and threw open the side door that lead from the garage into our kitchen. Patrice was soaked to the bone, sitting at the dining table and staring off into space.

"Where is John?" My voice sounded foreign, not my own. I have never used such a tone with my wife. "Where is he, Patrice?!" I rushed over and yanked her to face me. I shook her shoulders as a sob heaved out of my mouth. Her eyelids blinked as if in slow motion, but she didn't respond. She lightly tilted her head and looked past me, toward the hallway.

"I put him in the bath. She'd...well I think she left him outside for hours," Becky's grim voice came from behind me. Not turning back, I hurried to the bathroom to find my son. My vision blurred and I fought back the urge to vomit as I took in his bright red skin. The sounds of his cries hadn't registered until that very moment. They echoed, bouncing off the hard surfaces of the bathroom. His tiny fists were clenched tightly as he let out tired weeps, kicking his chubby legs in the water.

"What do I do?" I covered my mouth. It was hard to breathe.

"I can watch her while you take him to the doctor," Becky whispered from the doorway, her arms tucked into her slight frame.

"No. No, we can't take him to the doctor." If they saw what she'd done, how much more dangerous these episodes were becoming, they would take my son away.

"Is the boy alright? I only left him there for a few minutes," Patrice's gravelly voice rumbled from out of sight. An unfamiliar rage coursed through me as I shoved past Becky.

"I was so tired. I fell asleep," she continued, her body wobbled in the narrow hallway. Her hair dripping and clinging to her face.

"He was out there for *hours,* Patrice! He could have been abducted! He could have...he's *BURNED!*" I threw my hands up over my head, then froze. My eyes travel from her pale face and down her body that swells in the places I'd only seen happen once before.

"Patrice, are you?" I asked as a crack of thunder shakes the house. Becky sucks in a gasp behind me.

I hired Millie the next week.

AIMEE PINARD

John
Present Day

*I peeked through the 2-inch crack in the door to watch her.
Even at the tender age of five, I understood that her room was
forbidden. I needed something, but immediately forgot what it was when
I saw her. My mother. A beautiful mystery. I loved the smell of her
long blonde hair, like warm cake just out of the oven; which is ironic
considering she never baked a day in her life. She had piercing green
eyes that somehow felt like she could see into my soul, yet not see me at
all. When she entered a room, people would always stop and stare. It
was something my father both adored and loathed her for.*

*When she wasn't having one of her episodes, it was like
observing a butterfly fluttering delicately from flower to flower. When
she was, it was more like watching a wrecking ball swinging through a
glass room. We never knew which version we were going to get.*

This day was no different, yet it was.

*She didn't know I was standing there so I kept quiet, holding
my breath not to ruin the moment. Nothing seemed out of the ordinary,
until I watched my father come into view. His back was to me, so I
could not see his expression, but it was a surprise because he, too, was
not allowed in her room. My heart pounded in my chest, alerting me. I
should have walked away; this was adult business. But I so rarely had
the opportunity to watch my parents interact for more than a few
passing moments. I couldn't make out what they were saying, and I
jumped at the sound of her raised voice, "Please!" Please, what?*

My dad ripped his arm from her grasp which was unusual. My dad did nothing roughly or quickly. He was, at times, infuriatingly indifferent. If we hit a ball through the neighbor's window, he simply went to the hardware store for supplies to fix it. If I made the basketball team, he would offer a nod over the morning paper. He was mild, predictable, and my mother hated him. So, watching her tug at his arm, begging him to stay, was unusual. What struck me even more, was that he did not turn to exit through the door I was standing behind, he climbed out of the window.

I watched on as my mother fell back onto the bed, slumping over, tears streaming quietly down her splotchy face. We knew what to do when she was a wrecking ball. We knew what to do when she was a butterfly. But I'd never been a witness to that level of fragility. My dad often said that she was meant for more, that she was a movie star stuck in our small town. I spent many years of my youth terrified that I'd wake up one day and find her gone. Maybe that would have been better in the long run. Maybe not.

She heaved a heavy sigh and twisted around. I thought she'd decided to take a nap, but instead of laying down on her floral quilt, she slid her side table drawer open and pulled out a mirror. She set it in her lap and reached back in the drawer for something so small, I couldn't make out what it was. I made a mental note to check later. Her finger gently tapped out a white powder into a pile on the mirror. She tucked her hair behind her ear, hunched over the mirror, and held a playing card stiffly, scooting the powder into a straight line before sniffing it up loudly. I exhaled a small breath, as I noticed the immediate sag of relief in her shoulder, the way her forehead relaxed and her eyes closed. She was better.

I felt a small wave of panic as my nose itched with the threat of a sneeze. I tried to hold it, stepping back slightly to disappear into my room that was behind me. But I had stayed just a moment too long.

Her head jolted up, locking eyes with me. My heart hurdled into my throat as I waited. I stood frozen in my spot, watching as she slowly slid off the bed. The floorboards creaked as she walked towards the door. Towards me. I began to smile because for a split second, I thought she was happy to see me. She was smiling. Maybe she wanted to scoop me up and twirl me around to make her feel even better. Maybe she was going to sneak me in and tell me one of her stories. But as quickly as my smile formed, it vanished as she slammed the door in my face.

I wake from my daydream by the sound of my phone trilling off to my left. I pace over to the window where my desk overlooks the busy streets of Manhattan and pick up the receiver. "Hello!" I say, expecting it to be Victoria.

"Hello, John," says a voice I recognize, but one I definitely wasn't looking forward to hearing today.

"Hey, mom," I say flatly, hoping this will be a quick call and not one that drags out and ends up with one of us screaming and slamming the phone down.

"I just wanted to check in on you, make sure you're doing well. I hear you and Victoria are still going steady?" My mother doesn't call often and when she does, it's to guilt-trip me into visiting her. I have yet to agree. I absolutely do not want to introduce her to Victoria. She is the purest part of my life, and I can't give mother the opportunity to spoil what I've built for myself.

"Yeah mom, I'm fine. Vic is fine," I sigh and check my watch, "Do you need something?" I ask, half-heartedly concerned about her well-being and more out of obligation.

"I miss you John. It breaks my heart that the last time we saw each other, it didn't go so well. I'm clean, I promise. I've been doing the steps. I take my meds. I even see a shrink! Can you believe that? I'm not crazy anymore!" She lets out a self-deprecating laugh, trying to convince me that she was *better*, but we both know that will never be true.

"I'm sure you are doing fine, mom. I am just not ready to see you." I'm aware this crushes her every time I say it.

"Well, when John!? You're my son, don't you miss me?" She pleads, her voice shakes. It's funny because I'd never had my mother genuinely miss me or need me around without it benefiting her in some way. She never wanted to see me simply because she loved me. Honestly, I don't think my mother knows what that even feels like, to love someone or have the capacity to feel love. Not by my father, Ben nor myself.

"I'm sorry mom, but I'm just not ready to see you." A pause stretches from wherever she is, waiting for me to change my mind. "Listen...I gotta go. Vic is coming over soon, and I promised to take her out tonight." I don't give her a chance to protest. "Bye, mom."

It has been almost eleven years since I'd seen my mother, and it does eat at me every day at how we left things. I just can't bring myself to go see her, because it would mean facing all the things that she had done. All the things that hurt us. I finally have a good thing going, and it has taken so long to get here. The past still feels raw, as if it was only yesterday that we had the big fight after dad's funeral. He'd be so ashamed of how I handled things. I imagined him saying something like, *John, I've forgiven her, you should too.* Or, *You know she's not well, you can't hold something against her that she has no control over.*

I just can't help it. My father is a good man, or was. A better one than I am, that's for sure. She hit a nerve that day, and I just can't forget about it. Not this time. To be honest, in some ways, I have forgiven her. It's taken time. I did talk to Victoria's father, Marshall about that. He's always so wise. Like my dad, he knows exactly what to say to put things into perspective. We shared a few beers in his office one afternoon, and he asked why my parents never came around. Marshall is my boss, and over the last few years, we have grown close. So, when his beautiful daughter came to meet him for lunch one day, it was fate. I told him my father had passed away when I was in college, and my mother and I had a falling out and haven't spoken since. He didn't need to know the details.

"Well, don't you think that it's time to let some of that anger go? Try forgiving her for yourself." He had a point. I did need to move on, so I ended up calling her the next day. We had a nice conversation to start with. But like things always were with my mother, the more we spoke, the more she would bring up things that only made us angry. It's a work in progress, but we are closer to getting to a point in which I feel comfortable seeing her again. I guess that counts for something.

I don't talk to Ben as often as I'd like. He's busy with his entertainment career. He is in several Broadway shows and really fantastic at it. He and his partner have apartments in New York and San Francisco, they split their time between the cities when he's not working. I have made every lame excuse in the book for why I haven't been to either, but he'll call and check in every so often, despite his New York apartment being just down the island.

I don't blame him for the distance. After the childhood we had and the fact that I left, he probably felt abandoned. But I had to get out of there. If I stayed, I would have gone nuts, or ended up like Dad and I just couldn't have that end. I always promise him that I'll come watch one of his shows, and he politely responds back with, "Sure Man, anytime you want. I'll always leave a ticket for you." Ben is a good man, and I admire him as if he were the older brother.

AIMEE PINARD

Rick

Millie was a breath of fresh air. She allowed a level of security for me in knowing someone else was there when Patrice needed help. Patrice resented me for it, I knew that. I just didn't know what else to do because she was not a bad woman. She would never intentionally hurt our son. John and I needed her. The new baby would need her and we all went to great efforts to ensure Patrice remained happy and present. As much as she resisted the help at first—hurling insults at Millie about the way she cleaned or prepared meals—over time, we settled into a rhythm.

With a new baby on the way I hoped she would want to share our room again, but she didn't seem to have much interest in that. I stopped looking forward to waking up next to my wife, and was just grateful that we were dealing with a nice, long stretch without an outburst. If she preferred her own space, I respected that. I had failed her, after all. I saw the way she doted on Becky's daughter, how her smile seemed more genuine when the little girl was around. I had to do my penance. But maybe this time, we would have the girl she always wanted.

I allowed my excitement get the better of me, however. I tried moving her things back into our room, and what a mistake that turned out to be. She came home after running something over to Becky, whistling a tune as she strolled back to her room. I heard her rummaging and then yelled from out of view, "Rick! Where are my things!"

"Oh love, I moved it back! Don't you want to be back with me again?" I asked with a begging smile as I sprinted back to her room. Millie stood in the living room, pushing a vacuum and pretending not to be listening.

"No...I want to stay," her brows furrowed, "Absence makes the heart grow fonder, Rick!" She said with an anxious enthusiasm as she placed a hand to the large bump under her shirt. As much as I wanted her with me, I didn't want her to feel obligated. So, I dropped it. We continued living our lives as a happy family that retreated to their separate corners once the sun had set on our quiet street.

Aside from our separate sleeping arrangements, my wife was blossoming like I'd not seen since the early days of our courtship. She seemed happy again and as the months went on, we enjoyed life as we never had before. Ted and Becky introduced us to another couple who moved in down the street. Jed and Jane Patterson along with the Leonard's and us, started having regular get-togethers on the weekends.

They'd thrown Patrice a surprise baby shower, and she was the life of the party. On the days Patrice didn't have class, she would spend the afternoon at Becky's or take John to the playground. The holidays were approaching and she went out and bought all sorts of new clothes for all of us, even Millie. She looked as radiant as ever. I even noticed that she stopped smoking—a nasty habit she'd taken up after John was born. She thought I didn't know she was buying marijuana from the junkie two streets over, but I did and I never said anything because I had to choose my battles. She was doing so well.

Hiring Millie also gave Becky a break on watching both children. She was also an outstanding cook which was a nice change since Patrice had lost interest in cooking a while ago. I was so proud of the progress we'd made that I allowed myself to forgive the incident at the grocery store. When Patrice was doing well, she had the ability to convince everyone that it would never happen again. I foolishly believed her. Until she was close to the end of the pregnancy when she showed up at my office, red in the face and a bit out of sorts, rambling.

"He's an idiot. A pig...worse than a pig! He's a...a..."

I jumped from my seat, smiling tensely at coworkers who peered in with worried looks as I stepped around her large belly and closed the door to my office. She paced the small space, ranting on and making more barn animal references about her professor.

"But, what did he *do*, Patrice?" I asked, reaching for her hands and guiding her to sit in my chair.

"Does it even matter?! I'm done! I will never set foot on that campus again," she huffed and slumped back, crossing her arms over her chest.

I nodded as though I completely understood and reached for my phone to call the Dean. He informed me that Patrice had interrupted class and argued with her professor in such a way they had to excuse the other students. Under no circumstances would he be talked out of the probation, because it wasn't the first time...or the second. The *probation*. She had not quit school, they'd forced her to leave.

"See?! They're all sexist pigs," she mumbled sitting across from me. I sucked in a deep breath, contemplating how to fix this new mess, how to get Patrice back home.

"Oh love, don't you stress over that. Maybe this is a good thing?" I rubbed at my temples, my boss's shadow loomed from behind the blinds by my door.

"Why don't you go on home. I'm sure John would love that you're finished with school early!" I cringed at the face she made at the mention our son. Nevertheless, she sighed heavily and left my office.

When I returned, I found Millie and John sitting at the table having dinner and noticed Patrice wasn't home. John tapped his spoon on the table, bits of spaghetti noodles stuck to his cheeks as he stuck his slimy fist out at me.

"Da-dee!" he squealed.

"Hey, my boy!" I leaned over and planted a kiss to the top of his head and chuckled at the mess all over him. It made me happy to see him so content. "Hey-a Millie, where is my lovely wife?" I looked over to where she was scooping a bite of food into her own mouth.

"Oh, she's across the street. She said she was going to chat with Becky. She's been there a couple of hours," she answered with an eyebrow raised. Millie never spoke ill of Patrice, but her thoughts were like tiny whispers in the room. She did not think Patrice was a good mother.

"Oh, wonderful! I'm so glad she's getting out." I was so pleased that my pep talk helped. I sat down to have dinner, and a few minutes later, Patrice walked in with that award-winning smile on her face.

"So how was Becky?" I smiled up at her.

"Oh, she's lovely! I'm going to go wash up and come have dinner with you all!" she said and twirled around my chair. I was relieved to find her in better spirits. I didn't see this was just the calm before the storm.

Millie called me one afternoon, just a couple of weeks later, hysterical.

"Mr. Rick, Patrice has left the child in the car and he was barely breathing!"

"Have you called 9-1-1?" I spoke evenly.

"N-no, sir," she paused. "I know you've asked that I not do that, but please get home. NOW!" Millie was paid well enough to know that her discretion was important to me, to our family. The terror in her voice that time, told me that she might not be able to maintain it. It told me things were very bad this time.

I raced home as fast as my car would go, my heart pounded in my chest. I could barely breath as I took in the flashing lights, our neighbors standing on the sidewalks or at their front doors, watching, waiting.

"Where is he? Where's my son?" My voice sounded foreign in my own ears, the panic choked my words. A paramedic solemnly walked over to me, placed a comforting hand on my shoulder and assured me that John would be okay, but if it had just been moments longer, he might not have been. They advised they were going to take him in for doctors to give him a proper once over, but my wife would have to be evaluated.

"Evaluated? What for? She has some anxiety, but that's normal when someone is pregnant!" As I said the words, that seedling of doubt that had been planted so long ago, curved, curled and tightened around me until I could no longer ignore it.

However, hearing someone else imply that my wife was crazy, infuriated me. She made a mistake for heaven's sake, but she would never intentionally hurt our son or our unborn baby. Unfortunately, I could not convince them to let this slide. So, I reluctantly helped them escort Patrice into the ambulance, kicking and screaming, as our neighbors all stood with their mouths hanging open.

"It's that bitch's fault! I was just trying to watch The President! She should have been here to do her job! Let me goooooooooo! Riiiiick tell them to let me go! He was just napping! Rick!" Patrice screamed. Her eyes were large and blank. It terrified me.

My whole body went numb as I had flashbacks of Gaston's Grocery. I looked up and saw the pity in everyone's eyes. The heat index had been 100 degrees that day. John could have died. I watched the paramedics carry his limp body into the ambulance. Taking in the whole scene, I knew that this was it. All the wonderful playdates, birthday parties and card games would end. Even the idea of youth sports would be a strain now after this. I'm not a very religious person, but I begged God that night to make things better. To forgive Patrice, to forgive me for whatever wrongs we have done and allow us one more chance to get this right.

Millie handed in her resignation the next day. At the bottom, she affirmed that she had not called, likely wanting to collect her final check, which I gave her, because I knew she hadn't made the call.

I knew it, because I did it myself.

58

Becky

Rick was ever the doting spouse. His love for Patrice was all-consuming, while all she did was complain about him. Every time she came over sporting a new dress or handbag then proceed to whine about how he wouldn't let her work, or that he was so needy and wanted her around all the time, made me seethe inwardly. I thought about all the times I wished Ted would come home early or surprise me with dresses. I had to remind myself that he worked long hours and deserved that nap, or the late drinks with coworkers instead of relieving me of my duties, so I might take a bath without a child peering over the side of the tub.

Ted had been the quarterback of his high school football team. He was voted most likely to succeed *and* most attractive. He'd always been easy on the eyes, but he's only more handsome as he ages. We met during college, seated beside one another in history class. He asked to borrow my notes—because I was very detailed—and I was happy to share. We studied a lot together and wound up in his dorm one afternoon preparing for a big test. We were taking a short break, to relieve some stress, when his girlfriend walked in. Oops. That was the end of her. I can't help that we fell in love, or that I was too irresistible to ignore. She must have not been all that special to him. I knew how to keep him happy then and still do now. I certainly never found another woman in our bed.

I was the most beautiful bride, you know. Ted and I were like Ken and Barbie, at least that's what was printed in the paper. And although it took us a little extra time, he beamed with pride over Eve, over *us*. That doesn't happen as often lately. It is really tough having a baby who loves to snuggle with me every night. Nevertheless, he's a wonderful man and I am so fortunate.

After riding the Patrice rollercoaster for so long—I must admit—there was a slight sense of satisfaction as I watched her being carted off to the loony bin. Rick needed a break. I almost thought he started something up with that new maid of his, but I caught his eyes lingering on me on more than one occasion. I remember one time when Eve was still an infant, he dropped by to see if Patrice was over and walked right in on me breastfeeding! We'd both been embarrassed and agreed never to tell Patrice or Ted. It was a simple mistake. But I noticed the flush on his cheeks as he politely excused himself, apologizing about twenty times on his way out. He's so transparent.

I bet Patrice would have lost it though. With her shiny hair and short skirts, she could have never imagined her pitiful lapdog walking in on me and blushing like he did. I may have had twenty pounds of baby weight, but the girls were enormous. I'm sure any man would look. Ted loved them like that, all swollen and oozing with colostrum. He would cup them, squeezing with both hands, groaning with a primal desire. He didn't realize they were still very sore, but what woman would complain that her husband wants to be all over her?

60

Marie and Teresa came over the next morning.

"I guess the last screw finally came loose," Marie tutted as she plucked Eve's toys off of the couch and sat them delicately in the toy bin by the fireplace. It's her not-so-subtle way of reminding me that I didn't keep house as well as I once had.

"That poor little boy. Any word on how he's doing?" Teresa searched for a coffee mug in the kitchen behind me as I stood, hoisting Eve's sleeping body against me. Her soft puffs of air on my neck were little reminders of how lucky I was.

"I overheard the paramedic telling Rick that he would be okay. I'm just glad the maid showed up when she did." And I was. My relationship with Patrice had always been strained, but I would never have wanted anything to happen to John. He was such a good boy. "At least if she's locked away for a time, she can't hurt the new baby. She must be due any day now."

Marie and Teresa both froze in unison. Marie lowered herself onto the couch. "You don't think she was planning to...you know..." She couldn't finish the question, but we both understood the implication. This was not the first time she'd neglected John, and it was no secret that she wasn't thrilled about having another baby.

"Oh, Marie don't even say it!" Teresa slammed the cupboard shut, clutching an empty mug in her hand.

"Rick needs to take this opportunity to take John and move on to someone else," Marie added. She flicked her hand at Teresa to hurry along with the coffee.

"I don't know what he sees in that woman," Teresa confirmed.

My mind drifted to my own husband as the ladies spoke. How lucky he was to have a wife who loved him, cared for him, and bore a child as precious as Eve. His withdrawal from me had been slow. My need for connection had begun to grow. In turn, our marriage was suffering, and seeing Rick still so dedicated to Patrice was making me increasingly bitter. I was able to be self-reflective enough to recognize that.

"Do you think she would try to harm her unborn child, Becky?" Teresa turned to me, holding out a cup of coffee, the steam curling over the wide rim. I was so lost in thought, I hadn't even noticed her come up beside me.

I thought for a moment, considering all that I knew about Patrice. I'd been in their home, heard her say the most bizarre things. I'd also seen her be a loving mother, sometimes in ways even I fell short. Was Patrice capable of intentionally ending her pregnancy?

"I haven't a clue what that woman is capable of anymore." I shifted Eve, a string of her drool dripped down my chest. All I knew, was that my family meant everything to me. I would do anything for them.

Rick

Patrice was in the psych ward for weeks. I had to hire someone else to help with John and purposely chose someone new to our small town. Someone who didn't know Patrice and her history. English was Delores's second language which was even better. Even if someone did tell her about the episodes my wife had, she probably wouldn't understand and that offered some relief.

She appeared to be a good fit, because John loved her and our house always smelled of fresh lemons. Between work and visiting Patrice, I needed all the help I could get.

Patrice had regular sessions with her therapist, and they worked on navigating the things that triggered her. They tried to tell me that she suffered from something much deeper than situational anxiety, but I wouldn't hear it. Patrice was more than her poor decisions. I visited her twice a week, but in the last days of the pregnancy, she seemed to be on a decline—lifeless and withdrawn. A vast shift from the progress I had seen. Dr. Shawl advised that this was normal considering all of the work they had done, coupled with the medications in her system.

It wasn't until we'd reached the end of her stay when the doctor brought me into a different room before I went to where my wife waited for me.

"Mr. Adams, this is Dr. Fawn. He's been overseeing your wife's pregnancy during her time here." Patrice's doctor gestured to his left to a man who looked as though he hadn't slept in months. Heavy bags hung under his gray eyes, the whites webbed with spidery vessels. His skin was a dull khaki color, and I fought the urge to cringe at the thought of him being in an intimate space with my wife.

I nodded from her psychiatrists' wide face and narrow shoulders and turned to the man who was in charge of my child. "Hello!" I smiled. Something felt wrong.

"Mr. Adams," Dr. Fawn began. "I need to discuss Patrice and the baby's condition with you, and how you would like to proceed."

His words rolled together, thrumming in my head. I asked to wait to make any decisions. They advised that I could take until the weekend, which was only three days away. *Oh, Patrice. What mess have you gotten us in this time.* I signed all the paperwork and left the office. I did not return until they called to confirm she was cleared to leave.

Returning home had been difficult. I was tasked with relaying to everyone that although Patrice was well, quite well indeed, our baby was not coming home with us. Becky was kind enough to ensure no questions were asked, no gossip was to be spoken, and Patrice would receive the support and warm welcome she deserved. Losing her mind had gotten her labeled as a danger, a menace, while losing her child seemed to regain some sympathy.

Three years would go by and it was as if all the torment we'd faced together, never happened. For three years, that elephant in the room hid in the closet. People still knew it was there—of course they did—but the longer we went without any outbursts, the easier it became to ignore. She took John to the park, brought him on playdates, allowed Delores to teach her to bake a little. For three years, I watched my son grow and become interested in the world around him in new and intriguing ways.

I am not one to promote any form of mind-altering medications. I personally don't even like taking aspirin, but I have to admit seeing her more balanced than she'd been in ages was wonderful. And, although she still had no interest in sharing our room, she would slip in at night from time to time. I became instantly aroused at the sound of the door creaking open, knowing what was about to happen. Knowing she wanted me. The sound of her feet tip-toeing over to my bed, the feel of her body weight pressing down on her side of the mattress, the side I always leave open for her in hopes, one day, she will way to lay there permanently, all of it made my chest heave with desire.

It was clear, however the effects from being on the medication. We traded erratic mood swings for a good 20-pounds of weight gain which didn't bother me as much as it did her. But it appeared the more she put on, the more she desired me in a way she never had. One night when she climbed on top of me, I shuttered at the sight of her body draped in the silk nightie she wore. Her breasts full and drooping over my face, barely covered, as I reached a hand to tug a sleeve down to expose her. Patrice was magnificent at every size, in every way.

She whispered in my ear about how badly she wanted me, and the feel of her lips and breath against my skin alone, almost had me climax before we'd even begun. I ignored the smell of nicotine—she'd picked back up during her stay at the facility—rather focused on the hint of her shampoo and the sound she made as I ran my fingers lightly over her skin.

Those three years were heaven, and I have always thought of them fondly as the best years of my life. Because when it all came crashing down, I needed those memories to keep going.

Rick

Ben was born the following August. I didn't even know she had been pregnant. But when I paused to think back, I did notice her increase in appetite, and how her curves filled out her clothes more. Her skin glowed while she became repulsed by the smell of my morning coffee. How could I have missed the signs? I guess that didn't matter now. The damage had been done. She hated me again and blamed me for consistently failing her.

Before though, in the months following her return from the hospital, she suffered horrible night terrors. I was expecting some emotional flare-ups but nothing the likes of this. I felt the familiar rage from her that mirrored our earlier years of marriage, her disdain of having a son. Over time, her anger quelled. She loathed me mostly but was able to find ways to love me in small spurts. I could never make sense of it, could never understand because she wouldn't talk to me. Or maybe couldn't articulate her reasoning. In her eyes though, there was a knowing.

I found myself creating happier moments in my head just to get through the day. One afternoon, I knocked off work early and came home to find Patrice napping on the couch with the baby cradled in one arm wedged against the cushion, while John lay entwined in a blanket on the floor beside them. He had a toy tucked into the fold of his tiny arm, while a tiny pool of drool puddled under his cheek. Patrice's hair was knotted in Ben's unbelievably tiny fist. I couldn't even remember John being that small.

I stood there for a moment, basking in the glory that could have been. I closed my eyes, soaking it in and imagined that they were simply exhausted from running around the yard, playing tag as Ben rolled around on a quilt in the warm sunlight. That once they grew tired, Patrice scooped Ben up and raced John inside for some fresh lemonade, giggling as they sipped. Then, they would have curled up to nap as they waited for me to return.

I drew in a long, deep breath and slowly opened my eyes to accept the reality of our life. I saw an empty bottle of chardonnay sitting on the coffee table. A half-empty glass with a lipstick stain rested next to it. An Elvis album spun on the record player, the needle scraped on the end. Patrice's eyelids were gray and sunken as she snored. A cigarette dangled between her fingers that hung out over John's sleeping body. Little burn holes dotted the blanket that covered him.

I lightly walked toward them and plucked the butt from her hand and dropped it into the chardonnay bottle. I sighed again and quietly roamed to her bedroom at the back of the house and did what I never saw myself doing. I looked through her things. My pulse thrummed as I paced to her dresser and slowly pulled open the top drawer. There was a bowl full of cocaine, a smudged mirror, a marijuana pipe that had residue all around the mouth of it. I shook my head.

I moved to her closet and was hit with the smell of cigarettes and perfume. Her clothes neatly hung over her collection of shoes and the top shelf was stacked in boxes of things I didn't have the energy to snoop through. In her bathroom, I found a drawer full of condoms which we don't use.

I assumed she had stepped outside of our marriage a time or two, but I worked to ignore those intrusive thoughts. It was too painful to face what have become of us. Patrice only wanted to have sex with me when she was loaded. In the moments after she'd been sated, she would roll onto her side and tell me how much she missed me. But I knew better than to take it to heart because by morning, her eyes were cold once more. I ended our intimacy altogether when she began moaning other men's names.

However, no matter what she did, I honored my vows. I wouldn't betray her. Becky has put me in a precarious situation more than once, but I did not stray. I didn't even relieve myself to her image like I had planned, convincing myself that it was not infidelity.

I resigned myself to focusing on the boys. I was so proud of my sons. John had been a protective older brother and was so patient with Ben over the years. But as they grew, I noticed a difference in them. A strangeness in Ben that I never witnessed with John or most other boys. While they both were healthy and happy, Ben much preferred spending time in Patrice's room, running the fabric of her nice dresses along his cheek or trying on her shoes. John taught himself more masculine trades like fixing the sink instead of calling a plumber or repairing the lawnmower since I kept forgetting.

I'd moved up in my company since Ben's birth, which claimed more of my time. I hated to admit that suited me just fine, because with the boys needing things for school and paying Delores, we could use the money. But if I were completely honest, part of my distance was that Patrice had taken so much out of me that it became difficult to give anymore of myself to anyone else. She had been the light of my life since the day we met and slowly over the years, that light had begun to dim.

I was devastated the day I found those drugs in her room. It's bad enough that I had confirmation she'd been sleeping around, but to have drugs in the house where the boys could see, broke my heart. I tried to be her rock, holding on to the shreds of our marriage in hopes that we would find our way back to one another. I wanted so badly to keep her from the torment that haunted her, but all she did was fall right into the trap that her parents lay out for her. She appreciated nothing I had done for her, the sacrifices I'd made and the excuses I swallowed.

I wanted better for John since I had so miserably failed with Patrice, and watching Ben prance around in her dresses made me sick. It wasn't that he was a fruit, but I knew what it would mean for him. He'd come home with a black-eye more than once, and I often found his clothes torn or his backpack ripped apart. We've had to buy three in the last school year. One day I asked him as we sat down for dinner, "Ben, why does this keep happening?" Ben looked up with a worriless face.

"Because Dad, some people are just not nice." I stared at him for a moment and was taken aback by the poignancy of his statement. My eight-year-old child already knew the darkness of this world that it took me decades to grasp. He needed to maintain that strength because I knew John would leave one day. Even at the age of thirteen, I saw he was tired of catering to Patrice. And without having someone to lash out at, she would self-destruct. These boys didn't have the childhood that most would envy. Their mother stood in the way of any normalcy they could have had. It was what killed her.

Becky

Patrice always referred to Ben as *the one she got right*. It disturbed me deeply. Poor John had looked to his mother like a goddess for so long, and she dismissed him entirely over and over. He was almost five when Ben was born and I worried that with how little she cared for him before, the new baby would make him feel even more ignored. Of course, Rick says nothing. You would think watching his wife favor one child over the other would bother him, but nope. I attributed it to the loss they suffered with the second pregnancy. I imagine in her already fragile state, Rick was walking on eggshells more than ever.

I was surprised he even wanted to have another child with her after what happened. I mean, I could hardly look at her without seeing all the horrible things she'd done. I couldn't wrap my head around how he was able to forgive it all so easily. It took me a long time to see her as human and not the ego-maniac she was, but I did for the sake of the kids. John and Eve were so close, and the months I'd distanced myself from their family, Eve would stand at the window and cry for her friend. When I would stroll her down the sidewalk, she would bellow and reach toward Delores and John if they were outside.

In the time she was away, I began dissecting all the moments I'd spent with her, all the things I'd allowed myself to look past to avoid conflict. I became angry that Ted did not agree with my decision to keep Eve away.

"She adores John and Rick needs us, especially now," he said over the phone one evening. He was working late, again, while supper sat getting colder by the minute, again.

"As the parent, my job is not to cater to another child or another woman's husband. My job is to protect and nurture my own!" The defensiveness in my tone was even annoying in my own ears.

"Rick has no one, Becks." I could hear the convincing smile even through the phone, even though he had not used that smile for my own sake in ages.

"Yes, well...maybe *you* should go over there," I tucked the phone between my shoulder and ear and scrubbed at a stain in the carpet. "I've paid my dues."

So, when she returned, I had to admit the feeling was bittersweet. I couldn't deny the tiny bit of joy that swelled in my chest when I saw her embrace John as he raced toward her. Even from where I stood in the shadows of my front window, I could see she was different. But would it last? Apparently, she had a threshold, because the moment she'd found out she was pregnant again, I was afraid she was going to be sent back to the loony bin. Rick and Delores kept her on her meds, which only grazed the surface of what she really struggled with. Feeling trapped.

She alienated herself just as she had done before. I'm the only one who put up with her, the only one who made sure she ate and acknowledged the boys. Delores kept up with the house while Rick withdrew. It was infuriating that he wouldn't fight for those boys. But we felt sorry for them. Plain and simple. I had to rise above, because that's what a good Christian woman, a good neighbor and a good wife does.

Our friendship was never the same. We never quite got back to how we were before, but I still tried because I had to admit, I loved John like he was my own. One afternoon when all appeared quiet at her house, I walked Eve over with some muffins and tea while Rick and Ted were at work. Patrice was thrilled to see me as she peaked through her screen door. She hurriedly pushed it open and yanked us inside before I had a chance to rethink my decision.

"Oh, Becky! It's so good to see you, it's been so long!" She hollered as she brought the tea and muffins to the kitchen. She began rambling about what a delight Ben was. I smiled awkwardly and looked around for John, missing that boyish scent of grass and dirt. He'd long ago stopped running up to hug me, and I wondered if he was angry at me for being distant. I told myself that he was older now and preferred being with friends.

"I know dear, it has been a while. How are the boys?" I ask and smiled at Delores who flashed a toothy smile as she cleaned the sliding glass-door.

"Oh, they're wonderful, dear. Just great! Ben is a star student!" she twirled from the kitchen into the living room, her blonde hair swooshed over her shoulder. She rattled off more of his accomplishments—which couldn't be much considering he'd only begun third grade—while simultaneously alerting Delores of how she needed to clean the window again. My eyes moved from wall to wall, taking in the photos she'd framed, so very many photos of Ben.

Ben as a baby. Ben on his first bike. Ben with Eve. Ben and herself. Only one of John...standing next to Ben.

"Has John moved out?" I couldn't help myself. The words came out before I could take a breath.

Her face flushed, "Why, no! How silly, Becky, he's only a teenager," she waved her hand and giggled awkwardly. Delores rapidly scrubbed away, pretending not to overhear.

"I just wondered how he's been since you only seem to want to talk about Ben. It's like you went to that place and came out not wanting to be around John, or Rick for that matter."

A part of me will always despise her. I watched her face pale, and her mouth drooped down like a deflated balloon.

"All has been just fine, Becky...thank you for asking," she said through tight lips as she hefted a trash bag to the garage. The click of bottles like a blaring siren.

John
Present

I sit for a moment, staring at his tie clip, surrounded in the flood of emotions I feel when I talk about the parts of my past that I don't enjoy revisiting. I look to my left and see my reflection in the glass of one of the bookcases. I look like I haven't slept in years, and truly I haven't. Not well, at least. I need a shave, probably a haircut too. I'm greying around my temples and inwardly cringe at the way they spring out like coiled wires. I rub my chin waiting for him to say something so I don't have to, but I guess that's why he's here. I look back at his tie clip and then let my eyes wander over his arms. They're covered in thick, grey hair that pokes out of his wool sport coat. I flip my pocket watch in my hand over and over. His bald head shines under the florescent light, and when he nods I can see the spot of light travel around the top of it. He clears his throat, and I snap out of my trance.

"One of my friends is the head of the board for a major nonprofit organization that helps families in need get back on their feet. He's got a wife and kids, dog, the whole deal. They live on a few acres somewhere near Middleton now. My other friend took over his parent's company after they died and then sold it. He's resting on millions and moved out West. He dates models. We all keep in touch, but sometimes it's just painful to see what they've become and facing what I haven't." I almost feel a relief finally admitting this to someone. That I feel inadequate. I'm embarrassed that I'm not more. That I couldn't just get over my shit and move on.

"I don't understand. You're a successful man, John. You live in a penthouse in New York City. You run a successful advertising firm. You have a relationship with a beautiful and successful woman. What more do you expect from yourself?" Marshall says in such a sincere way, making me feel that he's genuinely concerned as to why I struggle with my self-worth. I ask myself the same question every day.

I've gotten closer with Marshall over the last few years, and he's my voice of reason when I need it. He is like a father figure now, especially since Victoria and I have gotten more serious. His wife, Sandra, sends me a birthday card with some sort of homemade confection every year. She never forgets. She used to be an executive at a major hotel chain and retired to be able to be around for all her kids. She also volunteers at the VA. Vic comes from good people. I hope to create that kind of life for us one day. I want to go to t-ball games and ballet recitals, but then I have panic attacks over the fear that I'll get the sickness, too. That I have it already. That my family will inevitably shoulder the burden of my demons. The darkest ones that even I am not fully aware of.

Marshall and Sandra would make for great in-laws. They've provided Victoria a wonderful life. She's told me of trips they would take as a family to the mountains for hiking and fishing. She and her sister are both successful in their own right. They are always checking up on their parents, even though they're still very capable despite being in their late sixties. I recently got to go on a trip with them to their home in the Hamptons. It became even more apparent that she is the woman I needed to spend the rest of my life with. At times, I feel so out of place around her family, but I yearn to belong. I desperately want to have a happy family. So, I have these talks with Marshall in hopes that one day, I'll feel comfortable enough to ask him the most important question I will ever ask anyone. I just need to know that once I say it all, once he knows the ins and outs of who I am, he still wants me in his daughter's life.

We've been together for almost five years now. We don't live together, although I know she must be wondering if and when I will ever pop the question. She's one of the top producing real estate agents in New York City. When we met, I had just landed this job, and I've done a lot for myself in a short time. Marshall respects how driven I am, but reminds me that I push myself too hard.

"I've just seen first-hand what failure looks like. And I don't want to repeat history," I reply, knowing that Marshall is also a man of integrity who—over the years—has had his own struggles with a work/life balance.

"Who do you refer to when you reference failure?" He asks, adjusting his glasses.

"I think they both failed. Both of my parents. I'm sure my father did his best, but he still missed so many signs. He could have helped her. And she...when she had the chance to help herself, she didn't." I feel my heart begin to race at the thought of my parents. How angry I still feel even after all this time.

Victoria has been the breath of fresh air. The piece to the puzzle of my life that was missing. She's warm, encouraging but strong and independent. She deserves a good man. Someone who doesn't have so much baggage. I know we would make wonderful parents. I think I probably talk more about our future children than she does, but I can see her eyes light up at the thought of it. It's a lot for a woman to consider these days—having to balance a family and a career—but I will be supportive of whatever she needs.

The thing is, she doesn't know much about my past, and I'm hesitant to tell her. Marshall is easy to talk to, which most might find strange, but our relationship is a unique one that has given me a chance to figure out what kind of man I really want to be. There are days that I want to tell him every sordid detail so that I will know once and for all if he will accept me. But where do I even begin?

Committing to Victoria is terrifying. I need to be proud of what I see when I look in the mirror before I feel deserving of her. I look forward to the day we can start fresh somewhere new and exciting, begin an adventure together. I'll make the rest of her life just as much of a fairytale that it has been up to this point for me. Lately, that future seems more tangible, realistic. Maybe I'll bring it up to her the next time she has an evening off.

I just hope my mother doesn't call today. It always puts me in a sour mood. I have asked many times for her to give me space, but she never listens. Then again, if I thought my mother was stubborn and ruthless before, she certainly won't start taking orders from anyone now. I don't hate her. It's one of the things I remember discussing with the therapist all those years ago. I had to forgive her, but I can't forget. I still can't help feeling bitter and angry when she calls and wants to reminisce. I can't keep going backwards. What I can't stand even more is how she paints her own picture of how things went down, instead of what really happened. I allowed it for so many years, but it just finally got to be enough. We all had had enough of it, and although I was probably a bit harsh with her, I couldn't help but feel good about it. Finally, no bullshit. No pretending, and I think she respects me for it now...maybe not then, but definitely now. She still has her moments.

Part 2:
Summer of '75

Rick

It was Thursday, May 15th, 1975, an important day. John's birthday. The last day of his senior year, and he was leaving. I stood on our back porch, beads of sweat dotted my brow as I inhaled the warm summer air. Our beautiful pecan trees towered over the expanse of our yard. I bought this house when they were much smaller. I recalled imagining Patrice and our future children collecting the nuts that would scatter the lawn every fall. Patrice never really liked to bake, but I would catch the boys storing them in buckets from time to time to sell them off to neighbors.

Patrice was inside, banging around the kitchen. She was intent on making breakfast, but we all knew that she would forego the mission very soon. I found John packing in his room the day before and felt the nervous energy that emanated from him. I didn't know what to say to my son. I hardly knew him. He said nothing about college to us, his future plans, but judging by the thick envelope that came in the mail weeks prior, he'd gotten into Columbia. How about that?

My coffee mug felt heavy in my hand as I took a tentative sip. There is never a good moment to discuss my own news, never a time where anyone else could matter more than Patrice's latest project or worry. I'd even had to make up a story as to why I wouldn't be at work exactly a week before. If I had told my wife that I had an appointment with an oncologist, she would have spiraled. Her mental state had become increasingly erratic over the last several years. I couldn't get her to stay on her medications. Delores grew tired of the outbursts and quit. My parents had both passed within a few months of one another and I'd almost missed the funeral services because Patrice was having a fit. Even Ted and Becky were keeping their distance, claiming that life had simply gotten busy.

Life. I wonder what that word truly means anymore.

"Rick! RIICCKKK!!!!" Patrice's voice reverberated of the sliding glass door behind me. A few birds fluttered from the tree. "I need help finding the damn bowls!"

I closed my eyes for a moment before I turned to go inside. Ticking off the many regrets in my life. I apparently had symptoms for prostate cancer. I didn't want to jump to conclusions, because I knew that these things can often turn out to be nothing, but as I sat in that cold office, listening to the doctor explain the results of my tests, my life began to flash before me. His words ran together, an irritating buzz in my ears as I traveled back in my mind to the day I met Patrice.

The memory of when I was supposed to go right, but juked left and ran into Tommy Ratcliff, injuring my knee and ending my potential basketball career. This meant I met Patrice instead of taking out Donna Clarkson because I was at the laundromat instead of basketball practice. I was bewitched. The softness in her voice, the depth of her eyes, the intoxicating scent of her perfume. I fell victim to her. For so many years I was infatuated with everything about her and nothing else mattered but making her happy and creating a beautiful life together. But until I found myself sitting across from a stranger who was basically reading me my last rights, I had no idea what a horrible and life-altering decision I had made. I didn't even feel sorry for myself, but guilty for my sons. So guilty that I didn't pick a better mother for them, guilty that I didn't snap out of her spell until it was too late. Guilty that I may have played a part in what truly ruined her but most importantly...I felt guilty that I didn't feel guilty that I get to die and they're left with her.

I didn't tell anyone about the news, the boys didn't need to feel like they had to baby me. Certainly, John would want to cancel his trip and I wasn't having that. He needed to get far away from this bottomless pit of destruction as soon as possible. Now that I finally had the wool torn from my eyes and could see our life for what it was. I despised this woman. I worked so hard to love her and no matter what I did, and how many times I bailed her out of the most embarrassing of situations, it didn't matter. She is still who she is, John is still leaving, Ben is still a lost boy, and I am a dead man.

John

I woke to loud crashing noises in the kitchen. Rubbing the sleep from my eyes, I looked over and squinted at the clock. 6:09 am. Part of me wanted to believe that she was actually going to attempt to make breakfast, but I knew better. I rolled onto my side to look at Ben. His mop of blonde hair shot out in every direction. His mouth hung open letting out a rattled snore, while a bony arm draped over the side of the bed. Ben is five years younger than me but more mature than anyone I knew.

I had known for a long time that our family was different. We didn't have any strange religious beliefs or traditions. That would have been easier to explain. We lived a middle-class life like most everyone else. However, one evening when I'd had my friends Mickey and Roach over, they'd asked whose room was across from mine and Ben's. Roach hovered in the hallway, eyeing the pinks and oranges.

"You never told me you had a sister!" he'd grinned.

"I don't. That's my mom's room," I'd replied, flicking the lights on and tossing my backpack onto my bed.

"Your *mom's?* Your parents have different rooms?" Mickey asked, his brows squeezed together in confusion.

"Don't yours?" I'd replied as heat crept up the base of my neck. Humiliation throbbed in my ears as they both shook their heads *no*.

I knew that other moms didn't start ripping their wallpaper down because there were 'spies' between the seams. They didn't throw expired vienna sausages on a plate for dinner if Dad wasn't home to cook. Mom claimed the seventies were all about change and freedom. Our maid, Delores said the only thing that was noteworthy about that time, is that mom completely lost her mind.

In the weeks leading up to my eighteenth birthday, I'd felt a sense of calm. I was escaping. I'd gotten a scholarship. Roach and Mickey planned out a road trip to celebrate, and of course, Roach made sure we had girls coming along. One girl in particular that I'd wanted to get to know better since the moment she moved to our school. I made a point never to date. Dating eventually meant meeting each other's parents.

But that summer, I would have a full week before my adult life began. A full week away from my parents, away from responsibilities. I heard my mom call out for my dad who apparently was not coming, because the next thing I heard is, "John! Please come give me a hand!"

She hadn't cooked in years, and I knew she was already overwhelmed with the task, so I stretched and tossed a pillow at my brother to wake him up. Ben grunted and threw his covers back. I contemplated leaving before anyone woke up, not wanting to face the difficulty of saying goodbye to my brother, but I decided he deserved better. I would miss him.

We shuffled down the dim hallway, shielding our eyes against the bright lights as the kitchen came into focus. The little bit of optimism I'd felt just moments before, immediately drained from me. She had found and placed all breakfast items necessary and placed them on the counter. However, they were filled with nail polish bottles and were surrounded by every other item that formerly filled the cabinets and drawers. Ben and I stood there in horror as we both understood we would be late for school.

"Happy birthday to you," Ben grumbled under his breath and scratched his head.

She yelled from behind a mound of cutlery and cans of beans. "OH! It's your *birthday*?!"

I gave her a tight smile and lightly elbowed Ben. It was better that she hadn't remembered because now...

"I'm going to make *you* a cake!" She jabbed her finger at me. Her eyes were wild, her smile too big as she whirled around, knocking things over that crowded the countertops.

She hummed the birthday song and wiggled her hips to the beat. Ben and I stood there, watching her, waiting for her to come down from whatever cloud she was on. Ben stepped forward and found a box of cereal on the floor and proceeded to shove his hand inside and fist the dry, stale flakes into his mouth.

"John! What the hell are you standing there for? I need a hand already!" I snapped my attention back to my mother, who had clearly forgotten she was going to make me a birthday cake before 7:00 am.

"What do you need?" I sighed. Her hair that had once been bright and shiny, had dulled. She'd balled it into a wiry knot on the top of her head, and wore a stained sweatshirt over a too-short skirt. Her feet were bare and dirty as she kneeled on the counter top facing an empty cabinet.

"Well, this kitchen is just a mess. I's all out of order! I bet the Kennedy's don't live like this! I can't find anything, and I need the Christmas decorations down!"

My mother often rambled like this when she was having an episode. She was obsessed with the Kennedy family, hence my name. It was the only thoughtful thing she'd ever done for me. Ben was always her ray of sunshine, but I'm fairly certain she was hoping he would have been a girl. For one, she always said so and two, she was delighted when he wanted to play dress up in her old gowns that she never wore anymore. We called days like these *episodes* because back then, manic depression didn't really have a name yet—she was just crazy. My mother was crazy and everyone knew it, which made being a teenager in a small-town complete torture.

"Mom, it's May. Little early for Christmas decorations, don't ya think?" I started to slowly put everything back in the cabinets. My father's form appeared, then disappeared from view in the square window above our kitchen sink.

"Well I like Christmas time better! It puts everyone in such a better mood, don't *you* think?" she paused, but not for me to reply, she was blowing dust off of an old can of soup. "Now, please help me look for them honey!" she twirled around picking things up and placing them somewhere else.

"Ben and I have to get to school. We don't have time to look for decorations." I don't offer to help her later. She doesn't know that I'm leaving. Ben nervously shoves more cereal into his mouth beside me. His pajama pants are several inches above his ankles, and he's missing a sock. "Is there anything that isn't expired that he can eat for breakfast?"

"The decoraaaaaations, John!" She was growing impatient.

There was no use trying to talk her down. My mother had exactly three speeds. Comatose, teetering on the edge of sanity and this...and this was not to be touched. I robotically continued to put things away, knowing full well it was in vain. She had likely been at this all night and would probably continue until she passed out.

I was a little relieved because at the rate she was going, she would sleep through the afternoon and—hopefully— into when Roach would pick me up that evening. As much as seeing her like this frustrated me, it still broke his heart, especially because my plan was to never return. She paused in the middle of all the disarray and finally looked up at me, "Oh honey, I can't believe I forgot!" My heart jolted in my chest. For a split second, my doubt had shifted into something else, something I rarely allowed myself to feel. Hope. I stopped cleaning and looked up at her. My beautiful, tormented mother. "I have Bingo tonight, so I'll need you to watch Ben. Your father is completely useless lately, so I don't want to rely on him. But don't worry! I shouldn't be too late and if I win, I'll bring you back a treat!"

She thought of me as eternally five-years-old, and all I needed was a treat to soften the blow of disappointment. My shoulders drooped with exhaustion. Her bingo nights were much later in the evening. I wouldn't be home.

Up until that very moment, I wasn't going to tell her that I was going away. Not only would she not remember, but she was not in the mental state for a serious conversation. To this day, I don't know why I said it. "I'm going to be gone for a few days, okay? The guys are picking me up after school."

A shadow passed over her face, followed by a long pause. My chest tightened as I waited for her to speak. Ben crouched into the hallway, still clutching the cereal box. Her head tilted slightly as she sucked in a sharp breath.

"Damnit John, this isn't a fucking circus! I don't need every Tom, Dick and Harry in my home! What if they steal something or break one of my nice vases?!" We had nothing that was worth anything. "For godsakes John, I have *bingo!*" I watched her hands tremble as the words rushed out of her mouth like she was possessed.

Ben didn't move. He was gauging how this one was going to go. If it ended well, he'd get to stay home from school and they would go out for ice cream or the cinema. Why my father was never concerned that she was driving around with his child in that state of mind never made sense. He would use his most understanding tone, "*She's your mother, son; she does deserve to have your respect even though she's sick.*" He always had so much more patience than she deserved.

At first glance, my dad didn't seem like much. He was over six-feet tall, and apparently played basketball in high school but quit when he injured his knee. I don't know what his aspirations were beyond that. As long as I could remember, his only passion was my mother. He never raised his voice, never swayed in the midst of her raging storm. He adored her despite all of it.

"You're right. I wasn't thinking. I'll tell them to come another time. Don't worry." I smiled at her knowing that she will have forgotten this whole morning by midday. Mickey and Roach would come and she'd say nothing of it. She would not be concerned whether or not Ben was home alone while she was gone. Something within me always longed to have a normal conversation with her. For her to ask how my day was and really give a shit.

She smiled back at me and somewhere behind her vacant expression, I saw she was coming back down to earth from wherever it was she'd disappeared to.

I spent the next hour cleaning the kitchen while she went on to rummage in another room until it was time to leave for school. The school halls would still be decorated from graduation a few days ago. I wasn't even disappointed that my parents hadn't attended. To be honest, I was relieved knowing they wouldn't come. There was a time that I didn't notice the looks my mother got in public. But the memory of our neighbors Ted and Becky glaring at her during eighth grade graduation stays in my mind as if it were something significant, but I never understood why. My mother had smiled and wiggled her fingers at them while my father sat staring forward. I now recognize that the way his lips were set in a thin line, his throat bobbing under his flushed face. He was embarrassed. Soon after, my mother stood up to sing the national anthem with my graduating class and when it was done, she began to bow and blow kisses at her audience. That was the last time they came to a school function.

Once I'd finished cleaning the kitchen, I went to double check that I'd packed enough and noticed her closet door was open. I walked into her room to shut it, and noticed it was empty. Her clothes, shoes, suitcases...gone.

Becky

Things were awfully quiet across the street on that last day of school. I imagined Patrice flailing around, rushing in and out as though she gave a shit. Like she remembered his birthday for once. Like all the years of nurturing that precious first-born; the scraped knees and snotty noses, hours of sleepless nights and birthday parties...all the memories gone by that would not be enough when that child becomes an adult seemingly overnight.

But Patrice did not care. She did none of the nurturing. She did not place a bandage on the bloody knees. She did not pull a tissue from her purse. She did not wake when her son cried out at night or bring him to birthday parties, nor did she throw one. That had all been the work of Rick and me. Would she even have thought to include me? Patrice thought of no one other than herself.

I fussed over Eve's hair as I tried to ignore looking out my front window.

"Mom, it's a little tight," Eve tilted her head away from me and placed her hand over her ponytail.

Wordlessly, I adjusted her hair, loosening it just enough without ruining the perfect, smooth base I'd provided her. Eve had lovely chestnut hair that ran down the length of her back. She would be graduating the following year and with each passing month, the walnut-sized lump in my throat grew larger and made it hard to breathe some days.

"Why don't you come out when we walk to the bus? I'm sure he would love to see you," Eve eyed the gift I'd wrapped for him. I'd spent hours at the store touching every fabric. I'd asked countless questions about the integrity of each one, wondering if they would stand against the harsher temperatures of New York's colder months. After I'd finally decided, had it specially wrapped and placed in my car, I suddenly felt silly. What 18-year-old man wants a stupid coat for his birthday? Of all the things I could have gotten him!

"No...I don't want to embarrass him. I'll just bring it over after school," I smiled and gave her a kiss on the cheek.

"He's leaving you know?" she replied, tugging on her backpack. "Roach, Mickey and some of the other girls who are graduating are going to some fancy ranch house. They are leaving right after school."

The words were a shock to my system. Was Rick aware that John was going away *with girls*?

"That's highly inappropriate," I managed before turning to the kitchen.

"He's going to college, mom. There are girls there," Eve teases. "I'm gonna miss him too. I'm sure he'll come back to visit." She threw me a comforting smile and reached for the doorknob. The morning sun peaked through the thick limbs of our tree, and I squinted through the glare and looked over Eve's shoulder to see Ben and John talking to one another as they exited their home. Rick's car was not in the driveway.

"You think she forgot again? Is that why you're so upset?" Eve paused and leaned against the door frame.

I furrowed my brow and shifted my weight. "It wouldn't surprise me if she did. And now, he's leaving." My lip quivered at the thought.

Eve walked toward me and threw her arms around my neck. I inhaled her scent and inwardly remarked on how it's changed over the years. How lucky I am to have cherished those changes instead of taking her for granted. I'd made myself that promise many years ago. A promise that if God ever saw me fit to be a mother, that I would always put my child first.

"He will come back," Eve reassured me and gave me a peck on the cheek. "I'll see you later," she added before turning to leave for the bus. I hurried to the window and watched as she bounded down the sidewalk to Ben and John, and my heart warmed at the sight of their bright smiles, welcoming her. I miss those moments. Just as they got to the corner, I spotted Mickey and that delinquent, Joshua—who goes by the disgusting name *Roach*—walk up to meet them at the bus stop. Mickey is a lovely boy, and I knew he would make his parents very proud. *Roach* was a bad influence however. I couldn't wait for John to be thousands of miles away from him. Eve knows to stay far away from the likes of that boy. I'll never forgive myself for not putting a stop to that trip the moment I found out. Could have saved everyone a lot of heartache. Or maybe not.

Sometimes, shit just happens.

John
Present

It's been a week since my mom has called and I'm left annoyed with my own discontent. I don't want to talk to her, yet when there are long stretches between her calls, I worry that she's disappeared again. I contemplate going down to the atrium of my building, but I decide to try and call Ben. It has been even longer since we've spoken and I feel a pang of guilt. I'm the older brother, he shouldn't be the only one holding our relationship together.

The phone trills once, twice, then goes to his answering machine. His voice sounds both familiar and like a complete stranger's telling me to leave a message after the tone. I don't. He won't call back. I blow out a long breath and tap my fingers on my desktop. The sound of rain pulls my attention to the window and I twist in my seat. I have never liked rainstorms, and for whatever reason, they always give me a deep sense of dread.

Vic loves the rain. She calls it "reading weather" and demands that no matter what we are doing, whatever the plans are, at the first hint of precipitation, we shift gears and curl up on the couch together with coffee or wine and she recites from her latest novel. I love the soothing sound of her voice. The way she expresses the characters' thoughts and feelings as though she feels them the same way. It has helped my aversion to rain. I remind myself that now, I have something to look forward to.

I stand up and walk towards the window now, press my palms to the windowsill and lean my forehead against the cool glass. My eyes close and try to calm my heart that beats faster the harder the drops pelt. Victoria's rainy day demands only help outside of working hours.

The phone rings behind me, and I don't have to pick it up to know who it is. Of course, she will call when I'm feeling anxious. My mom is nothing if not predictable.

Rick

I came home from work early. The house was eerily quiet the way it always was after Patrice came down from one of her fits. I dropped my worn leather briefcase on the kitchen table and tossed my car keys beside it. Led Zepplin echoed through the living room, and I followed the sound to John and Ben's room. Standing just out of their doorway, I peeked around the corner and saw John laying on his bed, his body comically too big for the twin mattress. I wondered why he never asked for something bigger, more fitting as he grew. Nevertheless, he would be leaving for college soon, and I assume those beds aren't much bigger.

My eyes caught on something moving to the right where I find Ben standing on a chair, twirling in one of Patrice's dresses. He was smiling and mouthing words I couldn't hear, like he was speaking to an audience. I closed my eyes and let the music whirl around my head along with the sound of Ben's skirt swishing against his bony legs. I wondered how much would change for them once I was gone, once this thing inside me was finished eating away at my organs. There'd been moments I've wanted to tell them, allow my boys a chance to process what was inevitably going to happen. I closed my eyes and sucked in a breath as I lifted my hand to knock at the door when a loud *thud* came from inside the room. I pop my eyes open to see Ben had fallen off the chair.

"You okay, man?" John asked, shooting up to a sitting position.

"Yeah, I'm fine. John, can I ask you somethin'?" Ben sat up rubbing at his head.

"Sure buddy, shoot." John swung his legs over the edge of the bed to give Ben his full attention. I watched my youngest son run his fingers along the frayed ends on the hem of his skirt.

"What will I do when you leave?" He asked continuing to nervously fidget. I winced. I hated myself in that moment of confirmation that Ben did not look to his parents for comfort, but his brother. Ben was a sensitive and kind soul who needed me now more than ever, and was losing out.

Ben was the spitting image of Patrice. He had the same mane of blonde hair and olive skin. His round eyes and long lashes gave him an exotic look which didn't do him any favors when it came to the teasing he endured from the other kids. He and John couldn't have been more opposite. Ted once asked if they were both mine when we were too many beers into a football game. I laughed it off, but I'd often wondered about that myself. But I'd done the calculations and chose to give Patrice the benefit of the doubt. It wasn't until I noticed how different he truly was, that I didn't so much question paternity, but Patrice's closer involvement in his upbringing than John's.

While Ben was granted the mothering and devotion that John wasn't, he was treated terribly by his peers. He found solace in Patrice's false sense of understanding and support. John however, avoided being in a room alone with her. He learned much more quickly than I had, that being loved by Patrice came at a price, and a costly one at that. Ben was still young and at an age that a mother's love was pure. John and I simply didn't have that kind of relationship with her. Not anymore at least. It's not something that was openly discussed. In fact, we didn't discuss much at all. So, for him to question John now, told me that even though he loved his mother, he knew she was not really a parent.

"Dad'll be here, don't worry." John cut the record off and leaned into his brother. "Is anyone pickin' on you at school?" he asked. My heart ached at the pain in his voice.

Ben hesitated before replying, "Frank Richards said I was...well, he called me that same name I told you before that you said was bad. But, then he said mom is a druggy whore...which is bad, too, I guess."

My mouth went dry, and I quickly stepped out of view so they wouldn't catch me eavesdropping. *It's bad enough that Ben is being treated that way, but for them to speak ill of Patrice to her own son...*and just as the thought entered my mind, I knew I was kidding myself. He recognized long ago that Patrice was not like other mothers, but that didn't mean it was okay for kids to throw it in his face like he had any control over it. I could feel my skin begin to heat with anger. But it quickly subsided. You had to learn quickly in our house that nothing lasted long. Everything is always changing.

"Next time someone says that to you or about anyone in our family, you sock them in the face, alright?" John's words shocked me. I'd never expect him to encourage violence. He'd never even been in a fight. I wanted to intervene and let them both know what terrible advice that was, and that it would only lead to Ben getting his teeth knocked out. However, if Ben was going to be the way he was, he would have to learn to defend himself.

"Alright John..." I could hear the apprehension in Ben's voice. A silence fell, and I took it as my cue to go heat dinner up.

Just as I reached the living room, I saw two figures out of the corner of my eye walking up to the front door. I cleared my throat. "John! Mickey and Joshua are here!" I refused to call the boy by that nickname. He was a rascal as a young boy and has only developed into even more of a bad influence now that he's driving. Joshua is not the tallest amongst other boys his age, but what he lacks in height, he makes up for in personality. He smokes, drinks, performs poorly in school and I've heard the rumors about how he is around the girls. Horrible character notwithstanding, they seem to fall for the smile and the long hair.

Mickey, on the other hand, comes from a good family. That kid is really going places. He is a beanpole with thick-rimmed glasses and the whitest-blonde hair I've ever seen. They're an odd threesome, but I have always appreciated their friendship with John. I can't erase what Patrice had done to him, the eternal scars that he's too ashamed to talk about, but having good friends is something I didn't allow myself as a young man. At John's age, I was focused on Patrice, on her happiness. All that bought me was a life of loneliness. I know John will be something great, and that greatness will have nothing to do with me.

John

There was a split-second where I considered backing out of the trip. A gut feeling that I wish I'd paid closer attention to. How could I leave my brother behind? Realistically, I knew that I couldn't protect him forever. I couldn't forego the scholarship opportunity, and frankly did not want to miss out on a week with Rose. I told myself that this would all work out in the end, that without me there as a buffer, Dad would be forced to do better by him. Ben was going to need guidance and confidence. *Parenting* that my mother was never going to be able to do.

"John! Mickey and Joshua are here!" My father's voice bellowed from the front of the house. My stomach churned as reality set in. They would anticipate my apprehension and remind me of all the reasons we set this up to begin with.

I grabbed Ben's pants off the foot of the bed and tossed them at his feet, "Put your clothes on. I don't need my friends having another thing to give me shit about." Ben obeyed, yanking them up his legs as he hobbled after me out of the room.

I bypassed my dad who was hunched over the stove, intently stirring the contents. I gestured for Mickey and Roach to meet me out back, then pulled the sliding glass door open and was met with the warm air and a slight breeze that rustled the leaves of our trees. Their voices were low as they spoke to one another walking side-by-side toward me. They've been my best friends since kindergarten. No one knew me better than those two.

Mickey is one of the most selfless people I know. He was the eldest of eight and often took on the role of third parent. His dad is a postal worker and his mother stocks groceries—so needless to say—they don't have a lot of money. Yet somehow, they're always volunteering at their church. If someone is sick, they're the first to show up with soup. They're the family unit I wish I had. However, in a lot of ways, Mickey and I related to one another. Having to take on more of an adult role at a young age forces you to view the world from another perspective, only it's like walking uphill in too small shoes.

Roach, on the other hand, got his nickname after he swallowed a roach on a dare in fifth grade, and it followed him. He also sells pot, so maybe that has something to do with it too. His dad owns a business in oil and gas down in Texas, but runs the company remotely so they can remain closer to family. They're people of means and Roach is...well, he's Roach. Not having had to shoulder much responsibility at all, he relies on the threat that his dad will stop the annual donations if his teachers don't pass him. I heard a rumor once that he had sex with the Vice Principle but he insisted it never happened. He lives fast and hard without the fear of consequences.

Just as they walk through the garage door that leads into the backyard, I tense at the sound of my mom's voice, "John! Ben! I'm leaving now! Please don't eat too much junk!" Her head pops in the doorway as she flashes a smile and trots over to her car in too high-heeled boots and a miniskirt. I hate how she dresses, especially for as simple an outing as Bingo. I see Roach and Mickey exchange glances and turn red when they see my face. I don't get mad. What's the point? She's putting it out there, and I'm pretty sure Roach is who sells her pot and other vices. Honestly, he's doing us all a favor. The higher she gets, the less likely she will harass me about finding the mice she thinks are in the walls, or rearranging furniture because the President might visit.

"My parents forgot my birthday again," I sigh.

"Yeah? Did you tell them you're leaving?" asked Mickey, no sign of surprise in his voice.

"My mom was out of it earlier, I can't talk to her about anything when she's like that," I say shrugging my shoulders.

"I'm sure your dad would be cool with it. Just tell him," Mickey offered before slapping at a mosquito on his neck. I could tell my dad, and he would probably be glad for me to go. I don't know why I didn't talk to him.

Roach seemed annoyed. He never understood how delicate any conversation was in our house, "Man, we're leaving tomorrow! The girls are practically dripping for us," he rubbed his hands together. He'd been working on getting in Mary Beth's pants for months. I rolled my eyes because he only wanted her because she was holding back. The second he was successful in the mission, he'd drop her and that would make for an awkward rest of the trip.

"I don't get it. I have the highest GPA in the class *and* I have a car but girls won't even talk to me. How does he get girls!" Mickey threw his hands in the air exasperated.

"Well—" Roach scoffed and tugged at his crotch. "That's because I gotta huuuuge..."

"Please do not finish that sentence," I held up a hand and squeezed my eyes shut.

"Fuck man! Maybe you should do something to get an edge. Driving your dad's old station wagon doesn't really scream, 'Hey baby come suck this!' But I do have something that can help you relax," Roach grinned.

"No, thanks. I'd rather not...and I don't want anyone to *suck me*," Mickey muttered curling his fingers in quotations. His ears turned a shade of red I didn't think was natural for the human body. I had to change the subject before Roach pushed it too far. Which he often did just to fuck with Mickey.

"So...tomorrow?" I interrupted before he could respond.

"Yup," Roach said, impatiently pulling his gaze from Mickey's clown ears. "I know you're ready to spend some quality time with Rose," he winked and spit at the ground.

Rose is the only girl I knew who had no interest in Roach. He tried and failed many times but she was not that type of girl. Not that I had any expectations of her. When I first saw her walking the hallways, her beautiful blonde hair swinging as if in slow motion, I felt instantly drawn to her. She's a junior at our school and became close with Jen through cheerleading. She was an only child and doted on by her parents, but didn't act like a girl who had everything handed to her. Jen always talks about how hard her parents are on her and how strict their rules were. It must be nice to have parents that care so much. I don't know what she told them about this trip or how she convinced them to let her go, but I wouldn't waste a minute in getting to know her better.

We'd spoken several times at school and football games, but it was impossible for me to date. She'd take one look from the front door and run screaming. One time in second grade, I wanted to give a girl a special valentine during our class party. My mom showed up saying how no little hussy was going to take her son. She ripped the card from the little girl, making her cry. I wanted to crawl in a hole and die. It took months for the kids to forget that. Although over the years, people started to pity me which was worse. Might as well just cut my balls off and roll them down the hallway.

So, I joined every sport. I figured if I was at least a star athlete, then nobody would give me any grief. It seemed to work along with making sure I always gave my parents the wrong day or time of any games or matches. I never wanted my mother to have another chance to humiliate me. Dad would always ask to come alone, but I really didn't trust him at that point. If Mom knew that he had any information, she would needle him until he spilled and then she would show up, and we couldn't trust her state of mind. I doubt she has even seen a report card. She has no idea I scored the winning goal at our state finals last season and the sad part is that I knew she wouldn't care. She has Ben who just got involved in his youth theater group at school. He still wants her there. And for some reason, she keeps her cool at *his* functions. It's almost as if the more *boy* I am, the more insane it makes her. She isn't allowed on the middle school campus after what she pulled at my graduation. Soon, she will have to start making excuses to Ben about why he can only perform his rolls at home for her because she's banned from the middle school campus.

I'm sure Dad would find some way to pretty up the truth. I swear that man would commit murder for her if it meant it would make her happy. I don't know why he catered to her so much and hasn't gotten sick of it. On top of her complete lack of maternal instinct, she's always dressing in skimpy clothes and he doesn't say a thing. He just quietly floats around the house indulging her when she's in a good mood or leaving if she's not. The man works himself like a dog and has nothing to show for it. Mom blows so much money on God knows what. Drugs. Clothes. Bingo. He doesn't even get pissed when she's snorting coke in her room with the door wide open for Ben to see. But I digress.

Mickey nudges Roach and gestures to the bag in his hand.

"Oh yeah, here you go man. Happy birthday!" Roach handed me a crumpled bag. I pull apart the opening, look in and fight against tears. I couldn't look up.

"Thanks guys! Really...this is great," I swallowed hard.

"Yeah well, it was a bitch to get back in shape, but we figured you were worth it," Roach teased.

"Happy birthday John!" Mickey smiled. I hate getting emotional, especially in front of them. It's difficult to go from feeling forgotten to having your two best friends plan something like this for you without getting choked up. They pretended not to notice as I opened it.

It's the old pocket watch we found when we were kids. We used to take turns keeping it safe and agreed that whoever turned eighteen first, got to keep it. Up until today, I had totally forgotten about it. We actually broke it running down some train tracks one day after Roach set off firecrackers in a neighbor's mailbox again. They must have had it fixed and placed a picture of the three of us inside. I remember like it was yesterday. We'd spent the whole day fishing at Blakeley State Park. Didn't catch a thing, except Mickey somehow fell into some poison ivy. We camped out, built a fire and roasted canned beans with Mickey's dad. It was the best day of my life and for these guys to give me a memory like that to hold on to, meant more than they'd ever know. When I returned home from that trip, my mother conveniently forgot where I was and grounded me from hanging out with them for three weeks. She called Mickey's house and berated his dad about kidnapping being a crime while my dad coaxed her off the phone and apologized. I struggle to look Mick's dad in the face to this day.

Rick

My stomach churned at the sight of Ben watching his brother loading a duffle bag into his friend's car. I should go hug my son...hug both of them. Nevertheless, my feet wouldn't move. I stood in the same spot John left me, stirring the chili I made and had no appetite for. I didn't ask where he was going or when he would return, and I didn't blame him for not telling me. I'm his father, but even he knows I hadn't earned the title. He made that quite clear in our brief interaction the night before. So much left unsaid, yet what would it have helped?

The sound of music was muffled through the closed front windows. I heard the car rev up and whispered my goodbyes as I ladled chili into a bowl for Ben to eat when he was ready. The rest, I scooped into Tupperware to freeze, but at the last minute, I made a bowl for Patrice too. She would be hungry when she got home, I'm sure. I left a note on top of it for her to microwave it for 30-seconds, stir, then add another 30-seconds.

The effort drained me, so I decided to take a nap even though it was already late. Becky recommended a book to me a few weeks before. If I found myself up late, maybe I'd crack it open. Maybe Patrice would be in a good mood when she came back from Bingo and would want to watch the late-nights with me. More likely than not, I'd need to help her into her pajamas and tuck her into bed. The one I had never slept in.

Ben moved from the front door once the boys drove away and sullenly shuffled to his room. There was a knock at the door, but I didn't have the energy to answer. If it was the postman, he'd leave it at the step. I no longer had friends who would stop by other than Becky, and I couldn't even face her. She would be mourning John's departure just as much. Secondarily, she'd know something was wrong with me. I'd successfully avoided her for weeks, and even I could see how gaunt my face had grown. My sunken eyes, the grey pallor of my skin. No. No, I could not face Becky.

Instead, I waited for whomever it was to give up. Once the coast was clear, I peeked through the sheer curtains and noticed a gift-wrapped box on the doormat. I opened the door and quickly lifted it from the step and saw it was a gift for John. I looked up to see Becky staring out of her front window and she gave me a nod, a tissue wrapped finger dabbed beneath her eyes. I nodded back in thanks and stepped away into my home. I left the box on the coffee table, a promise to myself that John would be back for it. I just didn't know if I would be here when that time came.

John

"You gonna talk to Rose when we pick her up, or are you going to sit back there like a creep?" Roach teased. His left arm hung out the window while his right kept the steering wheel steady. Mickey sat in the passenger seat and kept adjusting his glasses, a nervous tick because Jen was coming and anytime he's within a few feet of her, he looked on the verge of blowing chunks.

"Fuck off, Roach," I rolled my eyes despite knowing it was a genuine question. I clammed up when she was around. "It's not like it can go anywhere. As soon as we get back, I'm getting the hell out of that house," I added.

"Oh, it's goin' somewhere. It's goin' right in her—"

"Ooohhkaaay, Roach let's cool it. We are about to have ladies in here with us, and it's a five-hour drive. Offend anyone and it's gonna feel a lot longer," Mickey pulled his glasses off and lolled his head out the window, letting the breeze whip his hair out of his face.

As they continued busting each other's balls, I couldn't stop thinking about how I left things at home. Sure, my mom didn't remember my birthday and didn't care to acknowledge the end of my high school years, but she would eventually. She would, at some point, realize I'd left, and I could only imagine her reaction and how it would affect Ben.

I also couldn't shake the feeling that something was wrong with my dad. He'd been more spacy than usual, and I couldn't remember the last time I saw him eat. The further I got from home, the guiltier I felt and decided that once we made a pit stop, I'd call to check-in. I assured myself that I would see that things were just as I left them. That would have been better than knowing I'd caused more problems that Ben didn't deserve.

Just as we turned onto Mary Beth's street, Becky popped back into my head and how I selfishly did not say a proper goodbye to her either. I made a promise that when I returned to collect my things before leaving for school that I would go see her. More than my leaving ate at me when it came to Becky, was a strange conversation I had with Ted a couple of weeks prior that made me wish I'd made time for her before.

It was after an especially exhausting night with my mom. We were all left behind in the wake of her rage, and the next morning I felt hungover. My body physically ached with the tension. Per the norm, she'd stormed out and had not yet come back. I'd dumped the cocaine that she left on the coffee table one too many times and watched it dissolve in the water as it swirled down, spiraling into nothingness. Watching the bowl refill with fresh water, I felt a calming sensation wash over me. A simple satisfaction, and even though she would get more, I felt in control at that moment. So, I started to clean the rest of the bathroom. Once that was done, I moved on to my bedroom, then my mother's room, her bathroom, the hallway. I cleaned until my arms ached, my knuckles bled and the knot in my back unfurled. I felt sweat beading up and rolling down my face, mixing with my tears. I didn't realize I was shedding them until I finally stood and looked at myself in the mirror. What a sight I was. I finished my cleansing therapy with a shower. The water was so hot that it burned my skin. I scrubbed myself raw. Finally, I gathered all of the trash bags filled with our filth and heaved them over my tender shoulders.

Once I stepped outside, the bright sun pierced my eyes. I squinted, staring out onto the driveway waiting for them to adjust. I heard the door open behind me and when I turned, I watched my dad walk out with his briefcase. I don't know what he was doing while I was having my little meltdown, but I guess he figured I needed some space. But, here we were, moving on with the day as if what happened last night, didn't.

"Off to work?" I asked.

"You bet," he replied with a sad smile on his face.

We nodded our goodbyes as he lowered himself in the car. Carefully and slowly backing out of the driveway, leaving me in the quiet of the garage. I stood there playing back how he had propped himself uneasily against the back of the car seat as if it was almost painful to do. The strained look in his face that I could see through the side view mirror and the way he gripped the wheel to steady himself before shifting the car in reverse. Something was going on with him. Something aside from my mother. Something serious.

"Don't you need to get to school?" A voice startled me back out of my daydream. Familiar. I tried to think of who it was before I looked up, but before I knew it, he was standing three feet from me. Smiling that pretty boy smile that made me cringe. He was wearing a perfectly ironed shirt, no doubt Becky's handy work. His shoes shined obnoxiously and I swear the tick of his watch was even snooty. Ted.

"Uh...yeah, I was just taking the trash out," I held the bag up as proof.

"Rough night?" His eyebrows shot up to his perfect hairline. They lived so close that I'm sure they could hear everything that went on in our house in excruciating detail.

"I guess you could say that," I moved to dump the bags in the can, swinging them a bit too wide and nearly brushing the jacket draped over Ted's arm.

"She's an interesting woman, your mom," he sucked in a deep breath and let it out with a sigh.

"No offense, Ted, but you don't know anything about my mom." I hated him. I hated his 'neat and tidy' persona. I hated how perfect their life appeared compared to ours. I hated how he left Becky lonely at home to keep up that appearance while she not only ran their home, but ours too. I hated that he lived a stone's throw from our front door and my dad had to see him every day being a version of himself he couldn't be.

"None taken..." I could see he was trying to get at something, but I didn't care to wait around for him to sputter it out.

"Well...I gotta head to school, soo..." I pivoted awkwardly, hoping he would get the hint and go along his merry way.

"Can I give you a lift?" he asked. Never in my life has he ever spoken as many words to me as in that conversation. And now he's offering to give me a ride to school, which by the way, was walking distance.

"Yeah...sure I mean, I guess so," I shrugged. I did just take a shower, and it was pretty hot. It would be nice not to walk into first-period dripping sweat for once. I opened the car door and, as expected, it was as perfect as he was. Not a piece of paper left on the floor or a cigarette in the ash tray. It was only about ten seconds before he started speaking.

"I think you're a good kid, John. Well, man. You're a man now, I guess. I know, I mean, I don't *know,* but I know your parents have always done the best they can. That sounds condescending, doesn't it? We've lived across the street for almost twenty years, so you do get to know people pretty intimately over that length of time. Your mother...well she...she's special, John..." he rambled.

"Ted...you're not making any sense. What the hell are you getting at here?" I was never so glad to be pulling up to school.

"Right. Ah. I guess I'm just trying to say that your parents are, deep down, good people. Maybe not so much *together* but they are. I think a lot of people can be hard on your mom, and it doesn't make life any easier for her. But you're about to go off in the real world and I just want you to not carry this with you. Don't bear this burden. Because you don't want to be in your forties wishing you had been easier on yourself, or let loose, or just made different decisions at one point or another," he stared straight ahead for a while then turned to face me and smiled his *Ted* smile. "Have a good one!"

"Right on," I replied.

And that was it. Rounding off, probably one of the most bizarre weekends of my life. I mirrored his smile and got out of the car so fast I almost slammed my hand in the door. What the hell any of that meant, I had no idea. But if I had learned anything in my eighteen years, it was that even though you're an adult, you still don't have a fucking clue what you're doing.

John
Present

Today marks a very important day in my life. A pivotal moment where I took control of my own life almost seven years ago. It always comes with mixed feelings because it is also the day we buried my dad. I never really got to know him as more than the man who allowed my mother to destroy us. I remember only one conversation with him that carried any weight, and it was the day before I left on a trip with my friends. It was our last summer together, our last week of freedom before we all went our separate ways. I guess my dad recognized it as something special.

"I know I could have done better by you boys," he stood beside me as I shoved clothes into my duffle bag. I could smell his aftershave and the starch he used on his work shirts. I don't think he ever wore comfortable clothes. I didn't acknowledge his words when he paused. He tucked his hands in his pockets and continued. "I tried very hard for a very long time. I just couldn't fix her."

Of course, it was about Mom. It was always about her. It could never be about anyone else. I clenched my jaw as I searched for my toothbrush and toothpaste that were buried in the mess on my bed. I avoided looking over at

Ben's neatly tucked sheets, guilt flowing in and out in violent waves.

My dad rocked on his feet and cleared his throat, "Ben will be okay," he said as if reading my mind.

"Yeah, well, it won't be because of you...or her. He will be okay in spite of you." I roughly zipped my duffle, unsure whether or not I had everything I needed but desperately wanting away from the conversation.

I felt my dad still, the air stuffy in the dimly lit room. I finally looked up at him, my chest tightened as I took in how poorly he looked. "Will you be okay?" I asked. At the time I didn't know the whole truth, but I sensed something was off.

He offered a tight smile, his sad eyes moved from my duffle to my face. "I'll be fine. You go enjoy your summer," he placed a hand softly on my shoulder, "You earned it."

The phone rings and I groan, beginning to loathe the sound as it almost always comes when I'm not in the mood for her. Especially today, because while it marks a turn for me, it also holds the memory of our worst fight, the one that severed any chance at reconciliation. She keeps calling, though, as if she doesn't recall how awful it was. Like she didn't ruin everything.

I decided to tell Vic about that summer but have yet to find the right time. She is a little angry with me, I think. Her body language was stiff when she brought me in a plate of lunch earlier. She hates when I work through and likely annoyed that I'd done it yesterday as well. I think of my father and all the missed opportunities, all the times he chose work over us. I should do better, and I will. Because today is an important day. My reminder that life is too short.

AIMEE PINARD

Roach

The whole town thought Patrice was nuts. I mean, there were definitely times where I believed it myself. But then—with a little help from my grass—she would open up about her life, and I got it. A person can only take so much, you know? I told her to leave Rick, to tell John what she'd told me, but as time went, I started to think that maybe she liked the chaos. It gave her something...shit if I know what, but it did.

I felt for John, though. He grew up with so many puzzle pieces missing that he could never see the full picture. I didn't want to tell him about the things his mom told me. For one, I don't think he knew how much time we spent together, and two, I selfishly didn't want to risk losing out. There was something about Patrice that drew you in and once she got you, it was like the second she left, you instantly missed her. Makes me want to punch Rick in the face for ruining her like that, but from the looks of him, he isn't all that happy either.

Aside from her, Mick and John, I trusted no one. Most people hung around me because I had rich parents or drugs. The latter of which I only started selling when my uncle got arrested and his customers came to my house looking for him. It gave me something to do, and truthfully, I thought it would get my parents to pay attention to me.

Pathetic, I know. So, I started using, thinking that would make them see me. Only it didn't work, so I used more, and more until one day, Patrice found me face down in the lake and slapped me so hard that I swore she knocked a tooth loose. She told me that it wasn't stupid to sell, it was a lucrative business and I could invest that money, but dipping into my own shit was like taking the money and lighting it on fire. I'll never forget that night. She saved my life and I didn't want to fuck things up with the first person who actually gave a shit if I lived or died, so I kept her secrets. I didn't tell John that his mom was buying drugs from me, and I also didn't tell him when we started hooking up.

One evening we were laying in the back of my pickup truck. It was getting cold as the sun went down, but neither of us wanted to leave so we ignored the goosebumps on our skin and draped my leather jacket across our chests.

"I never saw myself in this life," she whispered. I wasn't sure if she wanted me to respond or not. She turned her face towards mine, plucked the joint from my mouth and brought it to her lips.

"What did you want?" I asked.

"Definitely not two kids and a husband right out of high school," her voice strained as she held the smoke before turning to face the sky and exhaling into the crisp air. "I wanted more from life and Rick was so...nice."

"Isn't nice a good thing?"

"Nobody wants to fuck the nice guy."

I chuckled at that. "Well...you kinda did fuck him."

"Yeah," she sighed. "I did."

"Did you ever love him?"

She took another long inhale and held it a while before exhaling and turning to face me again.

"My mother once told me never to fall in love. Love makes you vulnerable and if you're vulnerable, they'll hurt you."

"So, why did you marry him?"

"All the women in my family go crazy. My mother killed herself. Her mother killed herself. And I'm sure her mother killed herself. I wanted to try to avoid doing what they did that made them...not want to live."

"But you aren't killing yourself..." my body tensed as I spoke. I was anxious about what she might say.

She smiled. Her lips pulled so tightly into a grin that sent a chill down my spine. "Nope."

I could tell when days were particularly hard because she would ask for way more than her usual, and then she started to want harder stuff. Stuff I knew John probably *would* get pissed about, but what was I going to do? In a way, I felt like I was the only real friend she had. No woman that beautiful should be so deeply lost and lonely. Talking to her was like talking to someone who understood everything you said. She saw things in me that I couldn't see in myself and made me feel like I could do anything, be anyone. Then again, she was insane.

I was upset when I heard she got so pissed off when John brought up our trip. I really thought she would have been cool with it. She would have most likely been totally fine with Rick leaving, but not her precious Johnny boy. I was going to talk to her about it myself, but she just left. I checked at our spot before picking up Mickey, hoping she'd have left a note. Nothing. The caged bird had flown and we were all left behind as if we meant nothing. When I got to John's house and Mickey was helping to load his shit in the truck, he whispered to me.

"My mom left."

"What do mean she left?" I said, trying to ignore the tightness in my chest.

"She just fuckin left dude," John said shifting so Mickey wouldn't hear.

"Man, that's shitty. Don't worry, she'll be back. She always comes back," I said, not knowing if I was trying to convince him or myself. I was looking forward to this trip even more after hearing that. We all needed to clear our heads.

Mick and John had gotten into good schools while I hadn't even applied. I didn't know what my plan was after the summer break. I thought my dad would retire and let me take over the business, but when I asked him about it, he laughed in my face.

"You actually think I would have left our family business—our *fortune*—in your drug dealing hands? You would burn this place to the ground in a week!"

I knew I wasn't the smartest guy around or as goody good as John, but I thought at least my parents would have faith in me. I remember thinking of Patrice in that moment and fought the urge to punch my window out.

Roach

I honked the horn and waited for the girls to come outside. John was as quiet as always in the backseat, but I could hear him squirming against the leather seats. I rolled my eyes and slammed my fist against the horn again when they finally emerged from Mary Beth's ripped screen door. I leaned forward a bit to see past Mickey. My chest still felt tight thinking this might be the time Patrice left for good. With my only friends about to go their separate ways, I already felt my world crumbling. Patrice was all I had left, and if she was gone, too, what did I have left? It was strange because I had never cared this much about any girl before. But she wasn't just any girl, she was special, someone who I thought really cared about me. I thought back to one of the other times she talked about skipping town, and I'd begged her to take me with her.

"You won't get in trouble. I'm an adult! I can make my own decisions," I sat next to her on my tailgate at our spot on the lake. I stared at our pinky fingers just an inch from one another.

"Oh, Joshua...you know that I can't do that. Not to you, your parents...It would destroy John," she wouldn't look at me. She watched a bird glide across the water looking for fish.

"What would you do?" she asked, finally turning to face me.

"Well, what the fuck would *you* do Patrice?" I felt myself getting angry. I knew what she was doing, and I hated her for it. I hated myself for falling into the trap. "I'm here! I'm right here and I care about you, you know that, and I know you feel something, too! Don't try and lie to me!"

"Josh... you're so young. You think you have it all figured out. I remember when I was that ignorant to the world. You have no idea..." She trailed off as a tear slid down her smooth cheek. Age hadn't altered her yet. I wanted to brush that tear away, feel the salty water on my fingertips, but I didn't. Mostly because when she references her *real* life. Rick. It forces me to see things for what they were, and not what we pretended them to be on the lake.

"Don't bring my age into this. Age wasn't an issue when this all began. And I'm not the one who started this. Don't tell me Rick does for you what I do! Nobody can make you..." She slapped me, and I deserved it. But it was true. I felt used. I tried to push it away. I tried not to see that I was just a plaything for her, but here we were. And I resorted to low blows because it's all I had. Anger and pain.

"You can't say that! You can't do that, too! Okay!? That's exactly why I'm leaving. That kind of shit right there! I'm not perfect, I know that. But I can't keep living where everyone thinks I'm crazy, Josh!" More tears fell from her gorgeous eyes. It hurt me to see her like this. But she *was* crazy. She *did* do a lot of stuff that pissed people off or scared them. But she's right. I'm not the one who gets to say it. I'm her safe person.

We ended the conversation with her promising to let me know before she left. We fooled around some more and made out until I thought my lips would fall off. She scooted to the edge of the bed of the truck and slid off, her shoes crunched on the gravel as she turned and stood between my legs facing me.

"I don't want you to go," I said staring at the freckle on her neck.

"You always say that," she chuckled.

"I know. But this time, I just have a feeling I won't ever see you again," I watched her eyes for any sign.

"Maybe you will, maybe you won't. That's how I keep my mystery," she smiled and pulled away from me. And then she was gone.

She was gone and unfortunately for me, it looks like I was just another actor in her play that she chewed up and spit out like everyone else. I clenched my jaw and took a short but deep breath. She wasn't going to ruin this trip for me, and I knew that I, at least, had one more week where things stayed the same. Mary Beth was no straight-laced girl either, but it made more sense to try and get something going with her than wishing things with Patrice would be any different.

I don't know what I'm going to do after this summer. If Dad wasn't going to give me a job then I needed a Plan B. I wasn't too great at planning ahead, because I typically got lucky and things always just worked out in the end. I'm not naïve to think that my luck would last forever, though. I know that I don't have much of a reputation, and I knew better than to think that my parents would throw me a bone. My reality had become more and more apparent as the days went by, especially when my guidance counselor said, "Now Joshua...I know I don't have to tell you that money won't be able to buy your acceptance into most colleges...and although you have 'passed' your classes, it's not like you excelled. You weren't in any sports or other extracurriculars. What is your plan?" Poor Mrs. Benning. She still thought she could get through to me. The truth is, I couldn't think about my future. I'm not good at anything, and I ruined my chances at being an athlete.

Once they let me play in a couple games my sophomore year, and I was psyched. I had been practicing every day.I wanted so badly for Coach Reynolds to put me in so that my parents would see me play. I sat on the bench with my pristine jersey, spotless cleats and a handful of uppers. I needed the extra boost to help with my nerves. I tossed them in my mouth and a split second later I hear Coach's voice boom over my shoulder, "ROACH!" I froze wishing for once he hadn't seen me. I looked slowly over, waiting for him to slap his clipboard over my head. "You're up. Fuck this up and you're done. You got me?" Coach Reynolds had a way with words. I was so relieved that he hadn't caught me and quickly fumbled to grab my helmet.

As soon as I stood up, I knew I screwed up before I even went on the field. I could hear the muffled screams from my mom who was probably wasted off of her own smuggled cocktail. There was no turning back. I had to play. Blinking hard against the drugs already taking effect, I clenched my fists. My hands were jittery and I couldn't stop moving, which in theory is good for the position I played. But two flags and a score for the other team later, Coach pulled me. Literally. He came on field and yanked my mask so hard I swore I had permanent neck damage. Next thing I know he threw me down onto the bench expressing his hatred for my existence. I couldn't make out half the words he was saying and the next thing I know, I was puking all over his shoes. Needless to say, nobody trusted me after that, so why even go through the trouble?

I would really need to start fresh somewhere else because of the bridges I've burned. However, trying to get a recommendation or asking for a reference was a joke. Nobody trusted me, and I can't blame them. I'm not one of those entitled dipshits who thinks I deserve the world. However, I did think my own parents would at least help me out but if they never cared before, why would they start now?

"Josh, this isn't something you discuss now that you're graduating. If you cared about your future, you should have come to us sooner," my mom said matter-of-factly over dinner one evening. She barely even looked at me when she spoke. She just raised an eyebrow sharply, in the most condescending way as she pursed her lips and cut into her steak. It was like I was one of their employees asking for a raise.

"Yes son, this is your mistake and your mess to clean up. We have done enough of that and would appreciate you taking some initiative," Dad added with this 'attaboy' punch in the air like he was giving me a pep talk for my t-ball game. I knew, in a way, they were right. I should have tried harder, but I guess I just always wanted them to care more.

I wanted them to get upset when they found out I skipped class for a straight week. I wanted them to tell me what their expectations were, that I could have the world if

I just worked hard. They never did. My parents were too busy throwing parties for charity and taking pictures for the paper to print stories about how they are such a generous family. Generous to everyone but their own son. I have no siblings, and I'm almost certain I was a mistake to begin with. This is one of the reasons I can relate to John so well, we both know what it's like to be overlooked. The difference is John's mom is insane and my parents are just assholes. Regardless, I need a plan and I will spend my summer trying to figure out what the hell I'm going to do with myself when I don't have my crutches there to lean on.

The girls squealed as they tossed their bags in the bed of my truck and piled in the cab. John and Rose exchanged words, and I could immediately tell they'd be all over each other from here on out. We had an unspoken agreement that the second we started the drive, everything that happened on this trip would stay between us.

Jen sat in the back with Rose and John, much to Mickey's disappointment. She was nothing like her sister Mary Beth. For twins, they literally had zero in common. Mary Beth was your typical dumb blonde, and Jen was a Brainiac. She and Mickey were a part of the mathletes and the sexual tension could be cut with a butter knife, but if he got in her pants, that would be worth celebrating.

I absently listened to the rumbling of their voices mixed with Alice Cooper on the radio. I thought of where Patrice was while we turned onto the highway, and wondered if she was thinking of me. I thought about me and the guys and how we weren't kids anymore. Would we all feel like we'd grown up once the summer was over? Had my parents already converted my room into a new wet bar and cocktail area? If I, by some miracle, was going to get my shit together and get a real job, where would it be? Would I ever get married, have children, live in a nice home with a picket fence? Only time would tell. I lit a cigarette and popped it in my mouth, grinned and yelled, "Schoooools out. For. Summer!" Everyone started singing along, and I decided that I was done with all the what-ifs. And I was done with Patrice.

John

We drove for five hours until all the girls started to ask where the next gas station was because they needed to pee. I saw the gas tank was running low anyway and Mickey was prone to carsickness, so before he had to go through the humiliation of puking out of the window, it was a good idea to stop and stretch our legs.

Mary Beth and Jo quickly unbuckled and raced inside. I noticed their hesitation once they flung open the doors to the entrance. I wasn't sure exactly what town we were in, but looking around, there were no other stores, and the only other car must be the clerk who was working at the counter. I handed Roach a few bucks for the gas and walked over to the phone booth that was positioned around the corner, praying it was still in service.

I dialed the number to my house, hoping Ben would answer. It rang faintly four times before I heard a click and gentle breaths on the other side.

"Hello?" my father's voice was shockingly weathered as if I'd woken him from a sound sleep. It was just after dinner time. I'd never known him to doze off so early in the evening.

"Heya, Dad..." I wasn't sure what to say now that he was on the phone. "It's John, I just wanted to check in."

"Ah, John," he sighed. I told myself that the shitty phone was the reason for how poorly he sounded. "Trip going well so far?"

"Yeah, just a lot of driving and not much to see. Should be nice once we get there," I say.

"I'm glad you're doing this. Going on an adventure with your friends. You'll never regret it, son," he cleared his throat and then there was static on the line. I worried the call was dropped, but then I heard Ben's voice.

"John!" he sounded surprised that I called. "What's it like over there?"

"I'm nowhere yet, but I'll call with more excitement when we get there. Is a...is mom back?" I asked, already knowing the answer.

Ben snorts, "Nope," he lowered his voice. "Are *you* going to come back?" A flash of heat burned through my nerves. Ben was angry with me.

I kicked at the dry dirt that lined the edge of the gas station. "I should have talked to you before I left..."

"Yeah...you should have," he agreed.

"I uh, I got a job up in New York. My scholarship covers my tuition and dorm, but I will need to work." I ran a hand through my hair, anxious like I was talking to someone of authority and not my little brother.

"So, you aren't coming back."

I hated myself.

"Well, I need to come back to pack, but I will leave the next day," I made sure to give myself very little time between my return and when I had to leave.

"Figures," Ben exhaled and the static crackled so loud that I shouted asking if he was still on the line. I heard the girls talking to one another as they exited the gas station and Roach waved, letting me know everyone was ready.

"Listen, I'll call you when we get to the house. Okay?" I promised.

Ben waited so long to respond that I thought he hung up. I was about to do the same, when I heard his small voice through the receiver, "He's sick, you know?"

"Who's sick?" I asked, knowing exactly who he was referring to.

"Dad. He's sick. He took care of her when she was sick, and she left him," the unmistakable tremor in his voice made me queasy.

"Don't you worry about Dad. He's tougher than he seems," I offered, not truly believing my own words. "Look, I gotta go, but I promise I'll call soon. And if you need me to come home—"

The phone call drops and my stomach plummeted along with it. Ben had never gotten angry at our mother. He'd always seen the best parts of her, even when those parts hurt us. I suddenly felt so selfish, but I couldn't very well make Roach turn back on my account. I jogged back to the car and felt Rose's eyes on me.

"Everything alright?" she asked, true concern in her soft voice. Roach purposely turned up the radio and made an obscene joke to Mary Beth to distract her from what I must look like.

"Yeah, just haven't left home for longer than a day before. My little brother is worried," I said.

She smiled and reached over to squeeze my hand, "I wish I had a sibling. Must be so nice to know your brother misses you already."

I stared down at her polished nails that rested on the top of my fingers. Where our skin met felt like it was on fire while the rest of me was drained completely.

"Yeah," I agree as Roach pulled back onto the road. "Yeah, he's a good kid."

Rick

John and Patrice had been gone for two days. I watched my youngest son pace the house, helpless. I, too, am helpless. I ignored the calls from my doctor, and I avoided Becky at all cost. If she saw me like that—a fraction of my former self—she would surely have made me go to the doctor. But I knew that I was beyond help.

"Dad?" Ben called from the hallway. I had resigned myself to my chair in the living room. It's sagged permanently to the shape of my body and offers some comfort to my overwhelmingly aching body.

"Yes?" I answered but made no move to meet him where he was. I couldn't if I tried. I turned my head, wincing at the effort. I longed for sleep, but it was never restful.

"When were you going to tell us?" Ben emerges from around the corner. The light from the front windows made him glow as if he were an angel. My angel Ben. I hid my paperwork in my side table drawer. My intention was never to lie to my sons, rather let them understand after the fact what happened. I had nothing of value to leave them, aside from the house. Patrice took all the money. I still had some checks coming in from work. Not full pay with my sick leave, but enough to make ends meet. My death, however, would leave Ben and John comfortable enough. I'd gotten my life insurance policy drawn up once I realized my fate.

Patrice would be gone a while. I knew that much. She did what she always planned to. Suck us all dry until she had her fill. I always wondered when that would be.

"Don't...don't tell John," I said between struggling breaths.

"He deserves to know," Ben protested, his arms limply hanging by his sides. He tossed the manila folder onto the coffee table that had taken every last bit of my energy to scrub clean.

"What he deserves," the words scraped and rattled up my throat. I coughed. Ben rushed over to kneel beside me, worry aging his childish features, "is a life." I looked over to a small, framed photo that I kept on the TV tray beside my chair. I take a few deep breaths, preparing myself.

"She was pregnant with John here. I hold on to this because it's my last memory of before everything changed," I started coughing and gestured for him to hand me a handkerchief. We both ignored the tinge of blood when I pulled it from my mouth.

"Ben, I know I'm not much of a father, and I wasn't much of a husband, but I have always loved you all more than words could ever say. You're more of a man than I could ever be, and you accept people for who they are. You don't expect them to change to make your life easier. I won't be on this Earth much longer, and I just want to make sure that you know you've done enough. Don't stay here and rot away. You and John need to find your own happiness, be with someone who loves you and don't become what I have. I don't want either of you to feel obligated to stay with me. Whoever you become, know that I am proud of it."

Ben sat there, staring at the photo for a few more moments and finally looked up at me. The tears streaming down his face sparkled in the glow of the lamp across the room. My hope was that he understood what I was trying to tell him, and for the first time in as long as I could remember, my son slowly moved closer and gently wrapped his arms around my body. I felt him shudder when he noticed how thin I'd truly become, but gave into the embrace, knowing it might be one of the last times we will do this. It's odd knowing that you will die soon, but not certain when. We hugged and cried together for what seemed like hours. I was so tired. Ben wordlessly helped me to my bedroom and carefully guided me under the sheets.

"I'll stay until you fall asleep," he said, pressing a cool hand to my damp forehead. I hoped he would not grow to have any regrets about his life as I have. My eyes fluttered as I watched him take inventory of my bare room. The perfectly hung clothes in my closet. The dresser, neatly set up with my cologne and brush. Nothing was ever out of place. I imagine that in another life, I may have made a good husband to someone. My eyelids became too heavy to keep open, so I rested them shut, fearing what lay on the other side. I didn't know if I could ever be ready. I feel the bed give, the creak of the springs as Ben leaned over and pressed a kiss to my temple, "You weren't all that bad old man." Despite myself, a tear escaped from the corner of my eye and slid down into my ear. Ben brushed it with a tissue and slowly slid off of the bed and left.

John

As Roach turns onto the gravel road to his family's ranch, the car becomes silent. We were always aware that his parents had money, that they had more than one home, but seeing the expanse of land, the lake it sat on, house that stretched—what seemed—endlessly.

"Well J, if we didn't know you were loaded before," Mary Beth teased. I noticed that she didn't refer to him as Roach. Mickey gawked and silently shoved his glasses up his nose.

"Y'all gonna get out or what?" Roach grunted while opening his door. It creaked and groaned, almost slamming back into him. The truck was a piece of shit, always breaking down and more rust than actual paint covered ninety percent of it. I knew he was considering this as everyone fell back into whatever conversations they were having before we rolled up, but that was Roach. As much as he manipulated his parent's wealth to get some things, he didn't use it himself.

We made our way to the front doors which were over 3-feet wide, each. The glass within them was so clean that without the sun's reflection, you might not think it was there. We watched as Roach unlocked it and swung them open at once and were hit with a refreshing aroma of lemons and lavender.

"Mom had the maids come yesterday," he noted. "I call the master suite, ya'll can pick from the other four rooms. There's two on that side," he gestured to the left of us down a hallway that was lit from a row of oversized windows. "And two that way," he motioned toward the back of the house where another expanse of windows showcased a deck with a firepit surrounded by Adirondack chairs and a walkway down to the lake where a dock held kayaks on one side and a boat on the other.

"You have a boat?" Mickey said in a hushed tone.

"My dad has a boat," Roach corrected, dropped his duffle bag and strode to the kitchen where a stocked fridge housed tons of prepared dishes, beer, fruit and sodas.

Mary Beth turned and winked at Jen and Rose before sauntering toward the master suite. Roach eyed her with a grin.

"I'll take one on that side," I pointed to one of the first rooms he offered. "Don't wanna hear anything that's going on over there for the next few days," I laughed and made a move before anyone could beat me to it.

"Anyone want to go jump in the lake? I'm dying to get the road smell off me," Rose asked.

"Yeah, let me get changed," Jen called out. "Bunk together?" she elbowed Rose just as I reached the hallway.

———————————————————————

Once in the room, I tossed my things on the foot of the bed and fell back onto the plush comforter that also smelled as though it had been freshly cleaned. My sheets back home were scratchy and threadbare. I let my mind wander in all different directions.

Back home.

The job I will begin in less than a month.

My new life ahead.

College.

I closed my eyes and wondered where my mother was, whether she will go home and see about Ben. If she didn't, will my dad be able to take care of him or will I need to defer my scholarship? Can Ben come live with me if I don't?

My throat constricted with worry and the reality of what's to come suddenly felt so heavy while it was meant to feel like an escape. But that's my mother for you. Just when she sensed anyone getting too comfortable, she found new and interesting ways to fuck you over.

"Hey..." a soft voice purred from the door. My eyes popped open and a wave of heat rushed over me.

Rose.

"Hey, what's up?" I asked, sitting up. I blinked against the dizziness.

"Are you comin'?" Rose bit her bottom lip as she leaned her thin frame against the door. She was wearing an oversized t-shirt and if anything else, I couldn't tell. I laced my hands in my lap to hide the rising need.

"Sure! Yeah, just let me get my trunks on," I say, but she doesn't move from the doorway. "Did you need anything?" I add.

She blushed and tucked a strand of hair behind her ear. Her hair hung down her waist. She wasn't wearing make-up, so her freckles were more prominent. I had a sudden urge to kiss them.

"Nothing," she smiled before turning and disappearing down the hallway.

I quickly changed and raced out after her, eyeing her long, tanned legs. In the kitchen, Roach was handing out beers which Mickey hesitantly accepted. The last time he drank, it was whiskey we snuck from a box in my mom's closet. He spent the rest of the night puking. I'll never forget the smell.

Outside, the sun felt different, everything felt different. Roach started running and scooped Mary Beth up, cradling her as he yelped and cannon-balled them both off the dock. Jen laughed and took Mickey's hand, tugging him along. His whole body flushed bright red, but he ran alongside her. Rose turned to face me, flashing her big, beautiful smile, and reached down to pull that t-shirt up and over her head, flinging it behind her.

I swallowed the lump in my throat as I digested every curve of her body. I felt dizzy again with how badly I wanted her, and the beer sent a warm buzz through my system.

"Come on, let's get in there," her voice drifted around me like a lullaby. I looked out to our friends, splashing each other in the cool early-summer water. The water along the dock sucking and slapping against the boat. Then, Rose's hand crept into mine and I felt her lightly tug my arm. I told myself that this summer was the one that would change my life. I was going to take control and start deciding for myself what came next.

But for now, I would let Rose guide me. I pulled her into me and threw her over my shoulder, her warm legs pressed against my bare chest. She squealed and playfully slapped my back as I raced toward the water, and jumped in. I wished to hold onto that moment forever. If only.

John

Present

Marshall asked to meet me for lunch today, but I was hoping to wrap up some work before the weekend. Victoria is annoyed with me. When she brought in my coffee, she barely paused to give me so much as a sideways glance before leaving for work. My head is pounding, and I rub my fingers into my eye sockets until I see stars. Today is my birthday—and like clockwork—the days leading up to it have been sleepless and agitating. She wanted to make it special for me, had planned a dinner party and was upset when I'd asked her to cancel. Had I known beforehand, I would have told her that I didn't want to celebrate my birthday. In our years together, I assumed she understood as much.

The phone rings and I let out a visceral groan. I don't want to talk to *her*—but as always—my mother manages to call at the most inopportune times. I let it ring. Each trill seems louder than the last. I squeeze my eyes shut, waiting for her to give up, for the answering machine to kick on, for the ringing to stop. Marshall was likely going to try and talk me into the dinner party, advocating for his daughter's attempts to make me feel loved and important. What they don't understand, is that although my mother was who she was. I still had love in my life. It was not the kind of love they are accustomed to, but it was loving all the same.

I remember my neighbors, the Leonards. Eve was a little younger than me and so much of my childhood was wrapped up in memories of her family. Mrs. Leonard was more mother than Patrice ever was, and I wish I'd told her that. As stern and cold as she may have seemed to most, she'd been the one to pick up where my own mother fell short. The day of my eighteenth birthday I saw her in her usual spot, staring out her front window. I called her the neighborhood watch because she always knew everything that happened on our street.

Eve told me that they'd bought me a gift and that I should stop by before I left for my trip. She'd hinted that it would come in handy when I moved to New York. I promised that I would, and I fully intended on doing it but by the time we got out of school, I'd completely forgotten. It didn't occur to me until we were several hours away that I'd left without saying goodbye, and it eats at me to this day because in that short time away, everything changed.

John

Over the next couple of days, everyone had officially coupled off. Mickey had gone from a constant shade of crimson to a deep pink anytime Jen was around. Roach and Mary Beth spent a lot of time in the master suite, only emerging to eat and re-hydrate. Rose and I had not taken things as far as our friends. I wanted to respect her, and since I was leaving, I didn't feel comfortable putting her in a position to feel hurt or disappointed. But it was growing so difficult. Every moment I spent with her, I wanted to kiss her. I wanted to do more than kiss her.

The third afternoon of our trip was relatively quiet, and a summer rain kept everyone inside. Rose found a library of sorts in the room she originally shared with Jen before Jen decided to sneak into Mickey's room. Roach teased him about it, but he maintained that his religious views and morals kept him from taking it any further than kissing. Jen, Mary Beth, Roach, and Mickey found an old deck of cards and decided to play strip poker in the game room that was attached to the garage. So, the main house was left to Rose and me.

I decided it would be a good time to check in with Ben, so I found a quiet spot and stretched the landline to a leather chair that smell of cigars and expensive cologne. The

142

sound of the rain against the window at my back was soothing and helped calm my nerves despite not quite understanding why I felt so anxious to call my brother.

"H-hello?" his small, sleepy voice answered on the third ring.

"Taking a nap?" I asked.

"John! Hey!" he perked up. A shuffling sound crackled into the receiver then cleared. "Yeah, I was up late last night."

"Oh yeah? What's goin' on?"

"Nothing!" he said too quickly, like he'd been caught in a lie when I hadn't really accused him of anything.

"Mom back or somethin'?" I fingered the cord of the blinds, twisting the string around my index finger.

"No... she hasn't even called. Not that I thought she would. Just...feels like she isn't coming back this time." Ben sighed. "Anyway, how's the trip going? Do anything cool?"

"Yeah, it's super nice here. Roach's parents have a house on a lake. We caught a bass as long as your arm yesterday! Kayaked a bit. Grilled burgers." As I listed off our activities, a weight of guilt felt heavier and heavier on my chest. I knew something was going on at home that Ben wasn't telling me, and I couldn't even admit to myself at the time, I didn't want to know what it was.

"That's cool," Ben yawned.

"How's the old man?" I looked up as I said it and noticed Rose peeking around the door. A sweet smile played on her lips.

"He's fine. I'd put him on, but he's uh...he's napping too."

"Good...that's good," I said as a humid silence hung in the air, threatening to suffocate me. "Well, I gotta let you go. I'll call again in a day or so, okay?" I said half-heartedly and didn't even listen to his response before I hung up and bolted out of my seat, through the room and outside into the downpour.

The raindrops were warm and fat as they pounded against my skin. My feet sloshed in the puddles, the smell of wet grass and summer filled my nostrils as my heart raced in my chest. My entire body trembled with a feeling I couldn't name, and I wasn't sure if the rain was obscuring my vision or if I was about to black out.

"Hey..." her tone was comforting and steady despite having to raise her voice for me to hear. I fisted my hair on either side of my head as I whirled around to face her. My chest heaved and my body ached as if the very air I was breathing, was pressing in all around.

"Hey," Rose said more firmly, her hand gently reached out and clasped around my wrist. I blinked, instantly deflating as if her touch sent a blanket of calm over my body.

"I think there's something wrong with my dad, and he won't tell me." Just saying the words created more space in my lungs.

"I'm sorry," she replied, ignoring the fact that she was also soaked to the bone, her t-shirt clung to her body and her bare toes curled into the long blades of grass.

I shook my head because she didn't need to apologize. In fact, the only person that did, had no idea what she'd done. Blowing out a long breath, I gestured between us and we both chuckle at how ridiculous we looked. The sound of muffled laughter rang out from the game room several yards away, and we both didn't make a move to join them. But I also didn't want to go back inside the house, so I motioned toward the boat that had a small cabin. Rose nodded and followed me to the dock.

The boat bobbed and sloshed small waves as we ducked inside, the rain steadily pounded against the cabin but once inside, it felt cozy, intimate.

"Do you want to talk about it?" she asked, her shoulder brushed against mine. I laced my fingers between my knees and dropped my chin.

"I'm not even sure what to talk about. He knew I was leaving and purposely didn't tell me, so it can mean nothing or..." I didn't want to finish the sentence.

"Would you stay if you knew he was really bad off?" she asked, shivering slightly as she bit down on her bottom lip.

"I don't know. I feel like I should, but I also know he wouldn't want me to. But my brother is young, he needs someone there," my eyes flitted back and forth, searching for a sign to guide me in the right direction.

"What about your mom?" she offered.

"Ha...I guess you haven't heard about her," I glanced at her and acknowledged her innocent expression. "My mom has always needed parenting more than us, but she just took off before I left to come here so who knows if or when she will be back. It's all pretty shitty," I admitted, my cheeks burned with embarrassment.

"I'm sorry," she said again, twisting to face me. Her small puffs of breath against my cheek made my stomach hurt. I was so drawn to her, but I knew if I took it further,

I'd ruin everything. When I looked up, her big green eyes were trained on me.

"What are you parents like?" I asked, working hard to ignore the pout of her lips and the small freckle on the tip of her nose, and the way her breasts peaked through her shirt.

"Boring," she let out light laugh and looked down at her hands, picking at a hangnail. "They're older and super strict. I'm surprised they let me come on this trip. I had to tell them it was girls only. I feel like they have tried to shelter me so much because I'm their only child."

"At least they care," I countered.

"Yeah, well sometimes I wish they cared a little less. I'm not even allowed to date."

"That's unfortunate," I cleared my throat.

"Is it?" she looked at me now, her eyes darted from left to right.

"Yeah...I mean, I'm sure a lot of guys want to take you out," thunder rolled overhead and we both jumped. I instinctively braced an arm over her and when I did, I felt her heart thrumming in her chest.

"No, actually," her words were so soft if I were just an inch further away, I may not have heard them.

"Well...um...do you, I mean have you," I couldn't complete a thought, but before I could try again, Rose leaned forward and pressed her lips to mine. I was dizzy with desire. I cupped her head, and deepened our kiss. She moaned against me and hooked her arms underneath mine, her hands splayed across my shoulder blades. Her legs lifted and rested across my lap and I freed one of my hands to hold them steady. Her smooth, soft skin damp beneath my

146

palm sent an overwhelming wave of want through me. I got lost in that kiss until another loud drumming broke us apart.

"Well if the boats a rockin'!" Roach bellowed and let out a hearty laugh. "You know we got beds inside?"

"Leave them alone, J," Mary Beth scoffed, but winked at Rose who blushed and tucked her face into my shoulder.

"We were about to run to the store to get stuff for s'mores. Want to come?" Mickey said from behind Roach. "Just get out of the house for a little bit?"

"Sure!" Rose chirped. "Just let me get some dry clothes on.

"Yeah, I'm sure you got real wet in there," Roach teased and I flipped him the bird as I helped her up and out of the boat. The rain was letting up, and s'mores did sound pretty damn good. Rose and I walked back to the house hand-in-hand, and even though there was so much unknown at that time, I couldn't help just wanting to savor every bit of her that I could.

Rick

The house was beginning to smell. Without Delores, I simply could not keep up with it all. Performing any task took considerable effort, and I didn't want to force Ben to take all of it on himself. He was still a child, my last family member left. Fortunately, I made a few casseroles before I became too weak, and he had heated those up, washed the dishes and tidied up as best he could. But I soon realized, the smell was coming from me, and I could not bear the humiliation of my son cleaning his father.

John called earlier and Ben's face lit up at the sound of his brother's voice but as they spoke, I saw the recognition in his face. He was also reaching a realization. As much as he missed his brother, when he looked around, he didn't want John back here anymore than I did. Our eyes locked in a moment, wordless understanding flowed between us, and he chose not to tell John what was happening to me.

It wasn't until the phone trilled in the middle of the night, waking me from a fitful sleep that I feared John would meet his fate before I would. Ben showed in my doorway, a shadow in the dark hallway.

"Dad, it's John. He's been in an accident," his voice quaked, his own fear filled the room.

I cleared my throat and struggled to sit up, "Get changed."

"Y-you can't drive that far." I couldn't tell if he was asking or telling me, but he was right. I was in no condition to drive, and I had no way of contacting Patrice.

"Go wake Becky," I strained, tugging my legs from the tangle of sheets.

Ben hesitated.

"Hurry!" I yelled and Ben disappeared down the hall. The front door lock clicked and the sound of the door opening and slamming shut woke something inside of me. A burst of energy and adrenaline coursed through my veins as I sprang from the bed and threw a robe around myself. My fingers were numb as I tried to tie the belt around my waist and shoved my feet into my worn loafers.

When I reached the garage, I already felt winded and worried I might not make a reliable companion. But what other choice did I have?

"Rick! What's happened?" Becky ran up the driveway while Ted came rushing up behind her, his perfect hair disheveled from sleep.

"I-I don't know. Ben just got a call from the hospital where the kids are vacationing," I say. My stomach churned.

"Can you...obviously we will drive but will you..." Becky stammered. Even in the moonlight, or maybe because of it, she saw the writing on the wall when it came to me.

I swallowed and shook my head slightly. Ben stood to the side wringing his hands.

"I need to come."

Becky tilts her head slightly, her brows furrow but I appreciate that she doesn't protest. This might be the last time I see him. "Then let's go," she pivots to Ted, "stay with Eve. We will be fine."

Ted gapes like a fish and a large part of me wants to laugh, but that would be inappropriate. Ben swings the door of the car open and helps me into the passenger seat before getting into the back. Becky trots with purpose to the driver's seat, starts the car and backs out as though we are just going to the grocery store and not about to embark on a very long journey. But if I do nothing else with my life, I want John to know that I have never abandoned him.

Roach

I'll never forget the sound of my friends screaming as we hydroplaned off the road. The shattering of glass and crack of bone was an unnerving melody that will haunt me for the rest of my life. That, for more reasons than the obvious, was when all of our lives changed.

"Rose...Rose!" I heard John shouting desperately for her, but I couldn't turn to check on anyone myself. My body was jammed into the door, my seatbelt tight against my neck and pressing into my face. I could feel warm blood running into my eye, and the hand that I had sensation in, throbbed with every beat of my heart.

"Where is Rose?!" John gargled and choked.

I couldn't tell if it was Jen or Mary Beth that was crying from somewhere to my left, or right...the truck was on its side.

"I'm going to get help," Mickey's voice was eerily calm.

"Are you hurt?" someone asks, voices are starting to fade. Tears fall silently from my eyes.

"I think my wrist is broken, but I'm okay. Nobody move! You could make it worse if you are injured," Mickey instructed. "John, lay still!"

"Where is Rose?" I think John asks, pleadingly before I pass out.

John
Present

"Why don't you want to talk to her. Clear the air?" Marshall asks, his eyes are on a notepad as he jots notes for his secretary.

I blow air through my teeth, wondering the same. I am a grown man now and deserve the chance to let her know how much my mother royally fucked up my life, but at the same time, what would it solve? She's incapable of change.

"Because the last time I saw my mother..." my words trail off. I don't want to admit that, although my mother did a lot of wrong in her life, I did too.

Marshall's hand stills and he raises his eyebrows. I fidget as he calmly sits up straighter and waits for me to continue. He won't let me skirt around anything like Victoria does. That's why he's a good boss and an even better friend. It's also why I feel an immense obligation to be honest with him about all the things I otherwise would tuck away for the rest of my life. It's like a confessional, only I don't follow any particular faith. God has never shown up in my life.

"The last time I saw her, I was pretty cruel," I say just above a whisper. "It's not something I'm proud of. I hate that she has that over me," I tilt my head and feel the satisfying crack of my neck.

"We all do or say things from time to time that we aren't proud of, John," Marshall reassures me. But I don't think he has any scale to measure it to. His idea of wrong versus mine has got to be skewed.

He doesn't know my mother.

AIMEE PINARD

John

The harsh lighting woke me before the pain did. There were voices I didn't recognize mixed with ones that I did, but my eyelids felt like they were glued shut. It takes several minutes to remember what happened, and it rushes at me like a tidal wave.

Roach was driving, the rain had stopped but the roads were slick, and he lost control of the truck after hitting a pocket of oily water. Rose was next to me, but she wasn't wearing her seatbelt. I recall considering telling her to buckle up, but I didn't. One of my many regrets. Mickey was in front with Mary Beth and Roach – the last thing I remember seeing before I blacked out, was Mary Beth's body lunging into the windshield like she was nothing more than a ragdoll being flung across a room.

The voices drummed between my ears, my head pounded, and my arms felt leaden as I tried to tug them up to cover my ears.

"Whoa, look who's awake," someone said as I winced.

"Sorry," their voice dropped to a whisper. "You've suffered a concussion, but you're lucky..."

Lucky. I think as—whom I assumed was the doctor—continued listing off my injuries.

Broken leg, cracked rib, minor abdominal bruising. Otherwise, okay.

As I forced my eyes open, they scraped like sandpaper. I blinked and gestured for water. Out of the corner of my eye, a person slowly stepped forward and placed a cup with a straw in front of my face.

"Ben!" I rasped, then the reality hit me like a boulder as I looked behind him to see Becky and my dad in the corner of the room. My heart dropped at the sight of him, how horrible he looked after only a few days. Maybe he'd already looked bad, but with time away, it gave the illusion that he'd gotten rapidly worse.

"We just got here an hour ago," Becky spoke softly, worry lined her face. "You gave us quite a scare," she added, her lip wobbled as she sank on the foot of my bed and placed a hand on my good leg. A motherly touch.

I swallowed, "H-how is everyone else?"

The doctor said my friends were all fortunate as well, but Mary Beth and Rose seemed to have sustained severe injuries. Their parents were also here and advised me not to worry before he excused himself.

"Can I see Rose?" I asked and noticed the flicker of Becky's eyebrow. Ben still had not said a word, nor had he moved from where he stood beside me, still clutching the cup of water.

"I'll go see if she can have visitors," my dad offered. I watched him turn and shuffle toward the door, the effort to hold himself up was clearly a strain.

I look to Becky, "Is he not taking any medication?"

Her lips parted but no words came. She didn't know how sick he was and likely only found out when they decided to come here together.

"He stopped taking them," Ben offered, his body finally dropping into the small seat against the window to my left.

"Why the hell did he decide that?" anger bubbled in my chest, and I inhaled as deep of a breath as I could before the pain shot back like lightning through my body.

Ben shrugged, helpless.

"Can you talk to him?" I look back to Becky, pleading.

"That's not my place, John. You know that," she fiddled with my blanket, averting her swollen eyes.

"I think we all know your place in our family," I countered, her gaze shot back to meet mine just as my dad re-entered the room.

"Her parents are pretty upset, as you can imagine," his face flushed and glistened with sweat. "They didn't know you boys were on the trip. Th-th-they..." he tried, but his eyes grew wide, his mouth slacked as he fell to the ground.

Dad was severely dehydrated and was given fluids and forced to rest in a bed down the hall. I was going to talk to him, demand that he does what he can for himself so that Ben would have at least one parent. Not knowing his prognosis was also not going to fly anymore. All the cards needed to be on the table, but first, I needed to see my friends. I needed to see Rose.

Becky advised that Roach was sitting in a chair in the hallway, waiting to talk to me. She went to get coffee and the nurse helped me into a wheelchair so Ben could give me a stroll. We found Roach closeby, his arm in a sling and a bandage around his head. His dusty brown hair was caked in blood and disheveled. When he looked up, he appeared to have aged a decade.

"Man, I'm so sorry. I fucked up—" he began, standing up to face me as Ben wheeled me toward him.

I raised my hand to stop him, "That wasn't your fault. Just be glad we're all okay," I assured him. "How is Mick?"

Roach nodded, his eyes red-rimmed, "He went into surgery for a broken wrist. In recovery now, sleeping," he sniffed and rubbed at his nose. "Mary Beth..." he dropped his chin and covered his face with his hand, "I'll never get the image out of my head of her going through the windshield."

"Where is she?" I asked.

"In there," he motioned to the door a few feet away. "Her parents basically told me to fuck off, so I've just been waiting out here hoping they'll tell me how she is."

"What about Jen and Rose?"

"Jen's parents already took her home. Luckily, she only had some minor cuts from the broken glass, but nothing that required her to stay."

I waited for him to continue, and that familiar sinking feeling returned when he wouldn't look at me. "And Rose?" I pressed.

"It's not looking good," he didn't need to apologize, he wore it like heavy cloak. I knew how guilty he felt. "She apparently lost too much blood; they don't have a lot of what her type is. You should go see her," he bit at his bottom lip. I didn't acknowledge the tears that ran down his face.

"I don't think they want to see me either," I rest my head in my hand. It was still pounding, but I couldn't rest

157

until I knew Rose was going to be okay. Just as a thick silence fell, I heard a weeping from down the hall. Roach looked up and tilted his head toward the woman.

"That's her mom, you should go talk to her," he said. Before I could respond, Ben strained and began rolling me down. He had yet to say much more than what he'd spoken in my room. His feet tapped in a steady rhythm on the glossy floors. The wheels of my chair squeaking with each turn.

I watched the woman who seemed more of age to be Rose's grandmother than her mother, but she was dressed well, and her hair was in a neat bob, resting just below her chin that was dipped into her chest as she dabbed at her eyes with a tissue.

I cleared my throat for her to know someone was approaching, "Mrs. Higgins?"

She finished soaking her tears and looked up at me, her face open and kind, "Hello?"

"John. I'm Rose's...friend. I just wanted to say how sorry I am, and if there's anything I can do to help—"

"Oh, oh you've done quite enough," her sorrow morphed into rage, "My *baby* is in there...she is...and I can't," she began to blubber again, her shoulders drooped, unable to maintain the anger she so desperately wanted to feel.

"May I ask if she's going to be okay?" Ben finally spoke, stepping from behind me and walking cautiously over to Rose's mother. He gently cupped her elbow with one hand and guided her to a bench with the other.

She gulped, inhaling a shaky breath, "Rose has lost a lot of blood and they don't have enough here or any surrounding hospital. She needs a donor."

158

"Can you do it? Or her dad?" Ben asked. Mrs. Higgins looked up at the ceiling and closed her eyes. Tears fell down the sides of her cheeks.

"No...no we can't," she said with a finality that indicated she was not willing to discuss it any further. Ben nodded, his gaze shifting from her, to me, then back. I didn't speak and neither did he. I think we both understood that although Mrs. Higgins didn't want to divulge what came next, the circumstances made her feel a strange sense of privacy and vulnerability. Like we might be the only people to ever hear it, and it would have to remain that way.

She looked down at her lap now, her fingers folding the tissue into a tight triangle, "We adopted Rose. We were never able to have children of our own, and by the time we considered adoption, we were already old," she chuckled. "But then, one day we got a call. We didn't even have a pack of diapers, but we knew we had to say yes. We knew she was ours. And now...I can't protect her. Neither of us have her blood type," her lip trembled.

"Can I try?" Ben scooted closer to her and lowered to his knees.

Mrs. Higgins froze and turned to my brother, "She has a rare blood type, sweet boy. You probably won't be a match."

"Might as well try," he looked back at me and raised his eyebrows.

"I will test, too. Ro... Josh will, I bet," I lean forward and regret it, but I hope she understands our sincerity. I've only just had Rose for a moment, and I can't bear the thought of losing her. I can't imagine how pained her parents are after a lifetime with her.

"Thank you," she said, but I got the feeling she was already accepting the worst.

Rick

"Pardon me for sounding harsh..." Becky began, hovering over me, "but what the *hell* were you thinking? Did you really plan on foregoing treatment? What about Ben?"

She scolded me for a while, and I took it. Cancer might have been eating away at me, but even the little doctors had done made me feel like I could go for a jog around the parking lot, or a brisk walk at the very least.

I blinked and adjusted my blankets, relishing in how much she cared about my well-being and that of my boys. I thought of how different this would have gone had Patrice been here. Would she have even acknowledged me at all?

"Why are you smiling?!" Becky slapped her hands against her thighs.

"I'm sorry. I don't mean to seem ungrateful. I will talk to my doctors when I get home, but I want you to be aware that even with treatment, my prognosis isn't great." I have accepted that.

"But it doesn't mean you give up," she swiped at a tear and took a step toward me, her smooth hand slipped into mine.

"Dad?" John's voice called from the door. His chair squealed as Ben turned him into my room and rolled up beside me. I swallowed against the pain of seeing John so beat up.

"Heya boys," my mouth tugged into a tired smile, but he didn't return it. Becky planted a kiss on the top of his head and rested an arm across Ben's shoulders, guiding him out of the room to allow us privacy.

"When were you going to tell me?" he asked. There was no warmth in his voice.

"I'm sorry. I should have told you. I just didn't want you to put your life on hold for me. I'd done that myself for..." I stopped myself from bashing his mother. He sighed and held his head in his hands. I marked each cut and scrap on his skin and felt overwhelmingly grateful he was alive.

"I know," he looked back up at me and a comfortable silence fell.

"Excuse me?" a nurse with a bun so tight that her eyes were comically pulled back poked her head in. "John, the doctor would like to speak with you about your labs," she smiled, revealing a mouth full of braces which I found even more comical and wondered if the meds they had in my IV were making me a little loopy.

"So, you'll let me know about next steps?" John asked me as he nodded, accepting her help to wheel him out.

"I will." I cleared my throat and rested my head back against the pillow. "Just please don't change your plans regardless of what happens," I spoke to the ceiling, unsure if he heard me or not.

Becky returned with Ben who was clutching a bag of chips in one hand and a soda in the other. His eyes were sunken, his skin pale and I only then realized, he was still in his pajamas. I noticed that Becky had a strange look on her face, one that ventured beyond the scope of the obvious.

"What is it?" I asked, motioning for her to sit before she fainted.

"I'm not sure I... well I overheard something in the hallway that concerns John," she stammered. Becky never stammered. I waited as she collected her thoughts. She wouldn't make eye contact with me which made me feel quite nauseated.

"What is it? What did you hear?" my throat constricted, but the meds kept me from panicking. I wasn't even sure if this was a situation that required panic. I had grown so accustomed to the outrageous life that was living with Patrice, that I couldn't register what was truly noteworthy.

Becky still won't look at me, but I see her eyes dart to Ben who had not moved from where he stood, still holding his uneaten chips and soda.

"What is wrong with John?" my chest heaved as I demanded a response. She jumped at my raised voice and looked up at me.

"N-nothing is wrong with him," she swallowed.

"Then why are you so upset?"

"Ben, why don't you step outside for a moment," she looked over her shoulder at Ben who blinked slowly, as if in a trance. I anxiously watched on as he shuffled his feet and turned toward the door. Becky inhaled deeply then blew the air out, making her cheeks balloon.

"John is a match for the girl who needed blood," she laced and unlaced her fingers, then shoved them under her legs.

"Well, that's wonderful, isn't it? Her parents must be so relieved," I wasn't connecting the dots. I never was able to. That's why I was always stuck, wasn't it?

"You're not understanding, Rick," she leveled her gaze, suddenly going very still, very stern. "She has a rare blood-type. Her own parents are not a match. The girl was adopted almost seventeen years ago."

As the words flowed between us, I began to feel faint. Our deepest, darkest secret was coming back to haunt us. The one that I'd never wanted to revisit. Part of me wished I had not been revived in that moment, because having to face the truth, face my sons with it...

Well, that was going to be difficult.

John
Present

Victoria has been very cold in the last couple of days, and I'm starting to get the feeling that I've done something wrong. But what? I was finally wrapping my head around the idea of proposing, but with each day that she rejects me, the pit in my stomach grows. She hasn't been home in two days, and Marshall hasn't offered any intel on her whereabouts. I guess that's the blessing and curse of your boss being your almost father-in-law.

I remind myself that although I haven't argued with her, I also am likely not the most pleasant person to be around. Even with my mother finally slowing down on the incessant calls, just the fact that she does makes me agitated. And when that happens, coupled with my mounting work that I've been slacking on, I liken myself to an ogre who hasn't eaten in days.

Maybe I did shout.

I haven't eaten a solid meal in at least 72 hours. I was hungry and Victoria hasn't been cooking. I've been staying at the office longer and longer, telling myself it's to catch up on work when I really haven't done a damn thing. Marshall has noticed, but he's the kind of boss that trusts his employees which makes me even more anxious because my mom hasn't called. Why hasn't she called and why do I want her to now after being pissed off when she does?

Maybe I did push Victoria away.

Maybe I am to blame.

I am the not-so-perfect mixture of my parents. No wonder Victoria is keeping her distance. I'll have to make things right. I just hope it's not too late. I love her.

Rick

My priority had always been to get her well, and I vowed to do anything to make sure that I would have *my* wife back. If she wanted another baby later, it would be ours. Not that prick Ted from across the street. I should have been with Becky when I had the chance. Her beautiful soft curves underneath her thin gown she used to nurse in. Her luscious full lips and deep brown eyes. I should have done it, then maybe Patrice would have gotten jealous and realized what she was taking for granted. I knew she had been screwing around. Ted being one of her victims, but I assumed they would at the very least be more careful. I felt so betrayed. I knew she was not well and that we had so much rebuilding to do.

As I mulled over what had so violently been dumped upon me, I knew what I had to do. I had to put aside my pain and anguish to make things better. I was determined to fix her, fix us. I'd placed her in the best facility around and she was getting the best treatment available. The doctor and I had made the right decision to place the baby in more loving and capable hands. A nice couple from two towns over had been wanting a child for years, and I knew anyone who wanted something for that long deserved a shot.

Patrice was on so much medication at the time that it sent her into early labor, but the baby was healthy despite her lack of care for herself. She was a cute little thing, tiny but round and alert. She had Patrice's mouth. I wasn't able to be in the room, but as they placed her in the nursery, I watched her eyes roam around. Her limbs constantly moving and waving. I couldn't let myself get attached. This was not our baby. I signed the papers that night. They didn't need Patrice's because she was still considered unable to make rational decisions. The doctor promised that she would never remember. I would get my wife back and we would be happy again. I honored my vows and committed to making my family whole again.

"Are you sure this is what you want to do?" The doctor asked for the umpteenth time.

"I'm not sure about anything anymore. I used to be. I used to think that things were black and white. Simple. That the world worked in this smooth and perfect balance. But not anymore. Not now. But I need to be confident that this is right. I have to know that I didn't screw everything up. That I didn't ruin my family. That this isn't ultimately all my fault. So, no doc... I'm not sure. But I must be. For her, for my son and for that little girl right there." I wouldn't look at him. I just stared at the little baby. Not mine. In truth. I wanted that baby far away from us as possible.

After the big fight, the one that ended in Patrice's final exit through our door, I thought it was all over. I felt relieved. I could finally move on and spend my remaining days only worrying about myself and Ben. John, too, of course, but he was a man now. It seemed like the spell had been lifted, and I was free. Only, things with Patrice were never so cut and dry. Her mistakes were coming back to bite us and she was conveniently gone. Which was probably for the better.

Becky

After leaving the hospital, I could no longer look him in the face. I couldn't justify in my mind the notion that he would give away a child, even in those circumstances. He tried to explain to me his reasoning, but I wouldn't hear it.

"The baby wasn't *mine*, Becky," he'd said.

"So! John wasn't mine, and I helped you with him. I loved him, *still* love him!" Hot tears streamed down my face.

"That's different," his voice lowered, and his eyes jumped from me to his gray hands in his lap.

"How?! How is it different?!" I searched his face, but as usual, he reverted to the meek coward he was. He opened and closed his mouth several times, but said nothing, just shrugged his bony shoulders and kept his eyes downcast.

I stormed out, only stopping to make arrangements for them to have a ride back home and drove their car the five hours back, alone. I rolled the windows down to keep me from having to smell Rick. I focused on the yellow lines of the road and not the ache of my heart breaking in my chest. I could hardly stomach Patrice, sure, but I would never have allowed him to lie to her for all that time about her baby. That wasn't his decision to make. That action alone made me question so many other moments in the time I'd know their family. How often had Rick done things without including her, and what were they exactly? Was

Patrice the way she was naturally, or had he created the monster she became?

I dissected all of it on that drive home. I scrutinized what I knew versus what had been told to me. If Rick was so upset about this baby not being his biologically, did he ever consider that John also wasn't his? Or Ben? Was it because this baby was a girl and not a boy? Was she too sane during their births for him to have sold them off under her nose? So many questions that I'll never have the answer to.

I pulled the car into his driveway. It was late, the sun had long set and all that lit the road were streetlamps and the lights coming from my home. Ted must have been watching obsessively because he stormed out right as I turned the car off. It was only then that I realized I hadn't called him with any updates. He must have been worried sick.

A small part of me felt a spark of joy.

John

I was a match and insisted they take whatever they needed from me right away. I didn't want to waste any time, and I'm sure Rose's parents didn't either. It went very well according to my nurses. I was sent to rest back in my room after forcing every nurse to swear they would keep me posted on Rose's recovery. They all agreed and pumped me full of morphine so that I would rest.

Roach called parents, make sure Mary Beth had company after her own surgery, brought us flowers and fresh clothes from the gift shop. He promised to stay until we were all cleared to go home. Mickey had left once his father arrived and before he exited my room, he leaned over and wrapped his arms around my shoulders.

"I love you man and if you tell anyone I said that I'll kill you myself," he pulled back and winked.

"Yeah yeah, just make sure you get home safe and let me know how they like Jen." I waved as he left my room and almost immediately my nurse, Joyce, walked in.

"Am I going to live?" I joked and sat up.

"Very funny kid," she chuckled. "There's someone here to see you. Will you be accepting visitors?" she asked. I knew better than to think it was Rose, and Roach was just in here. A fleeting thought crossed my mind that it might be Becky, so I nodded and tried to appear like I didn't feel like

I was just hit by a bus. I prepared myself for the third degree she would likely be giving me now that she knew I wasn't going to die. But just as the thought of her entered my mind, dread gripped me like a vise. I don't know how, but I knew it wasn't Becky. The clack of her heels on the hospital floor, her chattering as if always in a hurry and then the smell of smoke wafted through my sterile room. My mother was here.

"Oh, my God, John! Are you okay?! What happened to you?!" She howled as she flung herself on top of me.

"I'm fine, who called you? What are you doing here?" I asked, really wanting to know who on Earth would call her.

"Well honey, I'm your mother. Of course, I would be called if you were hurt. Don't be silly!" she said half sincere, half insulted as she vigorously rubbed my arm and tucked the sheets in around my legs.

"Who called you," I asked again. She paused and bit on her lower lip. "Better yet, *how* did they call you?" As far as I knew, nobody had a way of contacting her when she left.

"Funny story, you see...it's best we get you out of here first," she says as she begins to fold back the blanket that she just finished jamming into my side, then reached to smooth my hair.

"No Mom. I have to stay here until they discharge me. I can't just walk out." I hoped she got the irony of my statement.

"Well, we need to get you out of here. You can recover at home, with me. I can take care of you!" She seemed unusually jumpy. I wondered if she had snorted something before coming up.

"What's wrong with you?" I feel my blood begin to boil and my bones tremor in frustration. "I'm fine! Everything is fine, just go! I don't want you here!" I yelled, hoping a nurse overheard and removed her from my room. I'd have done it myself if I could.

"Why all the shouting, John?" Joyce rushed back in.

"Get her out!" I glared at my mother. She paced back and forth and stopped suddenly at the foot of my bed.

Roach

I didn't know how to approach Rose's parents and apologize for what I'd done. But I also didn't know how to face John if she didn't make it. So, I sat by Mary Beth's bedside, trying to make her laugh and waiting to hear the news, whatever it would be. We talked about her plans once she recovered, and I promised to visit her even though I wasn't entirely sure that I would. As much as this experience had brought me down to earth, I didn't know that I could be the guy she would ultimately regret, the one big fat stain on the memory of the best years of her life.

"Why do you do that thing?" she asked, presses her fingertip to my eyebrow.

"What thing?" I smile and dip away.

"That thing where you think everyone is so much better than you?"

"Aren't they? I mean, you're all going to college, John has NYU on the horizon and all of your plans hopefully wouldn't include near death experiences, especially if I'm not involved."

"Any of us could have been at the wheel, J."

"Yeah, but it was me. It's always me."

"You keep believing that," she cleared her throat and adjusted her blanket.

"What do you mean?"

She licked her lips, and I brushed her hair from her face. "I mean, that if you keep pretending to be the fuck up, you're not giving yourself a lot of room to not fuck up. But nobody is expecting it. I kind of wish you'd stop so..."

"So, what?" I ask, my neck flushing.

"I don't know...I'd like to know that when I'm away, that we could, I dunno...try this?" she giggled, then winced.

"You know I don't do relationships," I leaned back in my chair.

"Yeah, I wish you'd stop sayin' that too." She patted my knee weakly. I could tell she needed to rest, so I kissed her cheek and walked out into the hallway. I noticed Rose's parents in the hallway walking toward me.

"You're Joshua, right? And you're close to John?" Mr. Mayfield spoke to me while Mrs. Mayfield stared through me as if I didn't exist. She looked terrible, which was expected after what has been going on the last couple of days, but right then she looked particularly removed.

"Yes Sir, do you need me to do anything?" I ask.

"I need you to keep John away from Rose," he said with a dry, expressionless tone.

"I don't understand. He just saved her life. Why would you do this to him?" I stood up straighter and planted my feet.

"There are some things that have come to light that he won't understand, and it's better for everyone if we sever ties as soon as possible," Mr. Mayfield bowed slightly and moved to escort Mrs. Mayfield away. Her face was pale, and her eyes stayed fixed to the ground. I stood watching them turn away from me, not knowing what to say or how to react. And then there she was, standing in the gap between their heads about fifty feet away.

"Joshua...oh my God I'm so happy you're here!" It took several seconds for my brain to connect the pieces. There she was. Patrice rushed toward me as I gaped at her, stunned. Flashbacks of the last time I saw her flew through my mind until I felt dizzy. She threw her sun kissed arms around my shoulders. I remained frozen. My feet were cemented in the ground.

"Patrice? What are you doing here?" I managed to force the words out when my body stopped holding me hostage. I tried to shove my own pain out of my mind. The pain from today and the pain she'd caused. Something told me that what I was struggling with was far less significant than the true reason she showed up.

"My son and husband were in an accident, why wouldn't I be here?" She looked genuinely stunned that I would question her.

I cupped the back of my neck with one hand and pointed towards Rick's door with the other. Patrice nodded and gripped my hand, tugging me along with her.

"Josh... there's something I have to tell you. Something that John doesn't know about, and you have to help me out with it, alright?" she said as her eyes darted around.

"Does it involve him?" I ask.

"Yes...well...and Rose too," she says pulling me into a private waiting room. I spot Rose's parents sitting in the larger waiting room cattycorner to ours. Mr. Mayfield is staring at us. I force him to make eye contact with me because I'm afraid to hear what she is about to say. All I knew for certain was that it would be heavy. I took a deep breath and turned my gaze back to her.

"Patrice, just say it. I will help however I can".

"Rose is my daughter...my biological daughter. And before you say anything, I didn't know. Not until recently. A few minutes ago, actually. I was shocked as well when they told me. I mean...how does someone have a baby and they don't know, right?! It's crazy, isn't it?" She laughed and spoke in quick spurts of words. I couldn't fully comprehend what was happening, what she was confessing.

"Patrice! Slow down...what the hell are you saying? John and Rose are brother and sister?" Holy shit, I was expecting just about anything but that.

"Not exactly," she twisted her fingers together. The rings on each of her nicotine-stained fingers clinked together.

"I had an affair right after John was born. I got pregnant and miscarried...at least I thought I did when I was...when they took me to...I wouldn't have given away my baby!" she crumpled into my chest.

"So, George and Ruth adopted Rose?" My brain couldn't keep up with what I was hearing.

"Yes. Rick placed her without telling me. You have to tell John!" her voice sounded rushed and desperate. "He won't let me in his room."

"Patrice, you need to calm down. John can't handle this right now..." and just as the words left my mouth, she popped up off me and gave me a glare that was so full of hatred.

All I could think in the seconds before she tore out of the hospital was that I hated whoever was the father.

178

Whoever I had to share her with that resulted in something tying them together, forever. Nothing we'd ever done had brought her back...but this did. And in the most insane and selfish way, I was jealous.

Rick

It was me who called her.

Technically, it was she who called me when she returned home after running out of money. Once she realized we were gone, she marched over to the Leonard's house to find out where we were. In an attempt to avoid a meltdown, Ted told her what happened, and she called the hospital. I told her not to come, that we were going to be fine and back home in no time, but she insisted. That was her way.

As much as I wanted to be angry that she showed up, there was a comfort to the cadence of her voice, the smell of her shampoo mixed with the outdoors. Ben tensed from his corner of my room, wholly overwhelmed by the events over the last couple of days. I watched his skin pale and his lip tremor and wondered if he had felt the relief as well when she left.

She'd burst into my room first...

"Riiiiick!" she sang, whirling in as though she'd never abandoned us. She flinched at the sight of me, then quickly recovered, "Oh, Rick what mess have you gotten yourself into now?"

"I told you, I'm fine. You shouldn't have c—"

"I'm sorry to intrude," a soft voice echoes from behind Patrice. I watch as she freezes and turns on her heels as if on a lazy susan.

"Well, you have, so now what?" Patrice retorts.

The woman tilts her head and twists her face, "Well, my daughter is down the hall in surgery. Your son just saved her life." The room became very quiet as an elderly man shuffled in behind her and gently placed his hands on her shoulders.

Patrice sucked in a breath, beaming with pride as she shimmied and replied, "Of course he did, my son is a wonderful person."

"He's also related to my daughter," the woman became stone, eyeing Patrice like a lioness on the prowl.

"Th-that's not possible," I choked from my bed, my tongue like a dried slug in my mouth. I thought I would have more time to work out how to handle this.

"It most certainly is," the woman countered. "And you are our daughter's biological parents." As she made that declaration, it was clear she'd only pieced together the puzzle moments ago.

Patrice, for the first time in all the years that I'd known her, was speechless. However, she swiveled back to face me in the most eerily calm way that I felt my skin heat with her piercing gaze. "What is she talking about, Rick?"

I knew she would never forgive me, but I accepted the loss of her so long ago that it hardly stung when she stormed out. Becky's anger at me had hurt more. Two wounded spouses longing for years to have someone love them as deeply as they loved in return. But in keeping my secret, I'd betrayed Becky, and it's another sacrifice I had to make to set things right. That secret had festered and created this cancer that's killing me.

I look up at Ben who straightens in his seat, his eyes fixed on me. "John is not to know about this."

Part 3:
The Beginning
of
The End

John

New York is loud and colorful. It's fast and busy and all the things that my hometown is not. My classes are interesting, and my professors give extra credit if we show up to their open mic nights. When I'm not in class or studying, I'm working, and my busy schedule has been my excuse for not returning home. We all agreed to keep in touch, but it became too easy to leave everything behind once we weren't physically around to hold each other accountable. I think about Rose often, more often than I liked to admit. Her parents refused to let me see her, likely still angry that we'd helped her lie to them about where she was going and with whom. I understood, I even respected how protective they were of her. It still stung. I didn't want things to end that way, but I'd always known it couldn't be forever. I wrote her a letter once. I wanted to know that she'd recovered well and didn't hate me, but I got no reply. I told myself that it had been intercepted by her parents, but a small part of me wondered if she did read it and didn't write back because she hated me.

I do hear from Roach from time to time when I call to check on Ben and my dad, who had been on hospice for about a month when I got the call. I'd just walked in from a long shift and slung my backpack onto my unmade bed. My roommate Frank, was sitting at his desk, crouched over a textbook, headphones over his ears. The phone rang and he hadn't even looked up. I picked up the receiver and before I heard his voice, I knew what the call was about.

"John, it's Dad." Ben sighs. His voice has deepened in the months I've been away.

"Is he gone?" I ask, suddenly feeling a pang of guilt. I should have gone home over the holiday break.

"Not yet, but it's probably a good idea to come home," he replied. I thought about how different everything would be if I went back. How Ben would no longer be the scrawny pre-teen I'd left behind. How my father would be even more deteriorated despite his last-ditch effort to reclaim his life. Would Becky want to see me? Would it be awkward seeing Roach. I'm not the same person I was when I left, and everyone else will be just as changed, and it irked me.

"Have you called Mom?" I ask.

"Yeah, she said she would come, but you know how she is." he said. My mother had never returned. She'd apparently met some guy in California, and they drove around in a beat-up Volkswagen, did drugs and who knows what else. She would call Ben every so often and make empty promises before going another stretch completely forgetting she had a young son and dying husband. Good riddance.

Two days later, I was on a plane headed to a place I didn't even consider home anymore. I arrive at the airport that is virtually empty compared to the overcrowded hustle and bustle of JFK. I stepped out the doors to wait for Ben to pick me up, deeply breathing the fresh air. It's strange to imagine that you don't realize how much you miss something as simple as this, until you have gone without it for so long. Inhaling this different, clean air was refreshing, but overwhelming. I stood on the curb with my suitcase inhaling and exhaling until I saw Ben drive up in our father's car. I watched him step out and was shocked at what I saw. He'd shot up several inches in the last year and is almost taller than I am now. He looked just like Dad, only different. A flood of emotions rushed over me as I threw my body onto him and hugged him so tight, I thought might suffocate him. I didn't realize how much I missed my brother until this moment. He pulled back and walked over to a bench, sighing heavily as he lowered himself down.

"What's going on?" I ask moving to sit next to him. Ben looked straight ahead and said something inaudible.

"What's that?" I ask leaning in closer.

"Dad's dead. He passed late last night. I'm sorry John." Ben turned to me and the look on his face was one I'd never seen on him before. A look of helpless release. He had taken on so much of the burden when I left that I think he was morbidly relieved that Dad decided to go.

"I'm sorry too, Ben." I didn't know what else to say. No words could sufficiently cover the gratitude I had for him and no number of apologies to cover the fact that I'd abandoned him, and Dad like I had. I'd focused so much on myself and had enjoyed every selfish moment, but that's the thing...it was selfish. *I* was selfish. And now my dad is gone.

Ben sucked in a deep breath and blew it out over several seconds. "Mom is here," he said. "Got in last night. Guess she cares a little bit after all."

I kept so many emotions buried away for so long, they all came boiling over. If I hadn't been sitting, I would have collapsed. I felt myself fall against my brother as I sobbed into his shoulder. He reached around and held my body as I hunched over uncontrollably bawling for what seemed like an hour. I didn't know how to explain myself. Where did I begin? Would he have understood? I couldn't stay here. I couldn't hold the burden of mom leaving and dad dying. On top of the substantial amount of guilt I felt, I realized I hadn't really known my father. I didn't know how he liked his coffee or how he preferred his eggs. I didn't know if he resented me not calling more often. I didn't know if he was proud of what I'd done for myself. I didn't know anything because I never asked. I was selfish and let my brother be the sole caregiver for our dying father for years. How he could sit here and comfort me, still trying to protect me right now? We sat there holding one another for a while until I looked up and saw a line of agitated people waiting to pick up their loved ones. "We should get going. Who knows what Mom is doing there alone."

John

An hour later, we pulled up at 'home' where Dad had been under hospice care. I walk in the house and already know she's there before I even see her. My mother had a presence like no one I've ever known. Everything looked the same, but also completely different. Ben quietly took my bags and walked them back to my old room. Before I had a chance to take a breath, I heard her.

"Well don't you look smart!" The sound of her voice penetrated my skull and made me grit my teeth, kind of like when you hear nails scraping on a chalkboard. It's amazing how this woman had the ability to dismiss a situation that most would find uncomfortable or painful and pretend as if we have all gathered for a happy reunion. She threw her arms around me as I stiffened and tried to lean away from the embrace.

"Come on, haven't you missed me?" She stood back and folded her arms as if annoyed with me. I was clenching my jaw so tightly that my teeth began to ache. Behind her, Ben exited Dad's room and closed the door behind him.

"I've called and they're coming to take him to prep for the funeral. We've scheduled it for tomorrow evening, that way we can have the weekend to sort the house," Ben said flatly as if this was a business transaction. That's what Dad has been reduced to and it was pathetic.

"Well, good. I need to get back to Don anyway. I just came to make sure you didn't need me for anything," Mom snorted whirling into the kitchen and poured herself a chardonnay. I whipped around and glared at her.

"What in the hell do you think we would ever need you for, other than to ruin something?" My mother stood perfectly still but wouldn't turn to face me. Ben sat on the couch, and I felt him brace for action.

"Nobody has ever needed you here. You show up, fuck everything up and then leave. It's what you do and if you had made any good decisions in your life, you would show some remorse." I was writhing with anger as I looked around and landed on a photo of her and dad sitting on the mantle. I grabbed it and threw it as hard as I could at the refrigerator. My mother jumped and moved away from the broken glass.

"Don't you dare, John! Don't you dare!" She pointed her finger at me and began to move closer. Her lips parted as she was about to say something else, but Ben jumped up and clasped his hands around hers.

"Everyone is upset right now. Why don't we go get some dinner and let John have a moment to process this?" Ben turned her to exit. He gave me a questioned look that I didn't understand at first, but he was likely angry at me for getting heated when it wasn't the time. As always, Ben maintained the level head.

After they left, I grabbed a beer from the refrigerator and chugged it. I needed something to help me face my father before they came to take him. I took the thirteen steps from the kitchen to his room. Thirteen steps I had taken so many times before. Thirteen steps that I would take for the last time. The door creaked as I opened it slowly. I knew I wouldn't be disturbing him, but I need to prolong this encounter. Each step took several seconds until I finally reached him. He was unrecognizable. His skin was grey and when I placed my hand on his arm, it was cold and clammy. His pajamas draped over his body as his bones protruded through the blue pinstripes. Seeing my father like this gave me a sensation I had not allowed myself to feel in many years. He was gone and I never really said goodbye. I had wished the whole plane ride that he'd be unconscious because I wasn't sure I could face him otherwise. I wasn't at all prepared to land in a world where he no longer existed. I knew I couldn't bring him back, but I could still talk to him. I took a class about spirituality that went over the idea of an afterlife. My professor said some people claim to be visited by someone who had passed and that it can bring closure.

I spoke as if my father may be standing right beside me. I thought maybe he lingered in hopes that we would be able to connect in a way that we never could in life. I told him about how I was doing in school and how I managed to maintain a perfect GPA in order to keep my scholarship. I told him about how I had already been offered some internships. I talked about the different jobs I held so that I would have a good savings for when I graduated. I wanted him to know that his hard work and dedication to our family had paid off. I had done what he had failed to do. I thought maybe this would give him peace somehow. Maybe it was an arrogant thing to assume but Ben and I were going to be okay because of him, despite my mother. I hadn't noticed until now how I had taken this man for granted. I think sometimes we don't notice the good in our lives until it's gone. I really didn't know what 'good' was. I had been angry for so long because of the relationship we didn't have, but never focused on the idea that he gave me what he could. He was fresh out of support for us because he had to put all of his energy into Mom. I could never fully comprehend that until now. After I unloaded the last year of my life onto him, I kissed his forehead and hoisted myself up off the bed and left the room, closing the door gently behind me.

I went to grab another beer from the fridge and made my way to the patio. The pecan tree casting shade over the yard that was littered with pecans. It's a small comfort, but my chest tightens with all the memories I didn't want to be mine.

"Hey, John."

Something inside me lifted as I looked to my left and saw Roach and Mickey walking over to me, hands in pockets. Once again, they had come through for me.

"Wow, Mick when did you get in?" I walk over and hug each of them. I knew Roach had paid for my father's care. I also knew he didn't want me to mention it, but I would have to find a way to thank him for filling in where I fell short.

"Just now. Roach picked me up from the airport," he smiled and kicked at the ground.

"So, how's it going up there?" I asked.

"Pretty great! Jen sends her best. She had to stay back. Finals week." Mickey shrugged. I hated how awkward it was with us now.

"Anything going on with you worth telling?" I turn to Roach.

"Not much, just playing the field. I'm thinking of selling the house and buying some land in Cali." I look at Mickey and mouth *Mary Beth?* He shrugs before Roach adds, "She's busting my balls to get engaged since this dickhead had to go and propose." he jabs a thumb at Mickey and my stomach churns.

"No shit! Hey, man congrats! I had no idea!"

"Yeah, well you would if you called once in a while," Roach scoffs and goes into my house and I see him turn toward the fridge and grabs a beer.

"Don't worry about him," Mickey gently punches at my shoulder.

"I should have been in touch more," I look back to my friend who showed up even though I've been a jerk.

"We don't blame you, John. You needed to get away. We get it," Mickey said as Roach returned with a beer for each of them. We each sat on the stone ledge on the patio and spent the next hour catching up. The tension dissipated and we fell back into the brotherly banter that had kept me sane for so many years. It made me so happy to see my friends were doing well and had full lives. The sun began to set and we turned at the sound of a car pulling back in the driveway.

"Mm... mom is back with Ben. He had to take her out because I kind of blew up on her," I snorted and took another pull of beer.

Roach flushed, "Your mom is here?"

I nodded.

"Well, I guess I better get you to your folks. I'm sure your mom has a 7-course meal prepared for you," Roach elbowed Mickey who laughed.

"See you tomorrow?" Mickey looked down at me.

"Yep," I sighed.

Back inside, Mom is putting on a record and Ben begins to pull out a casserole dish to heat up for dinner. The normalcy of it, the memories that come flooding back nauseate me. I feel sick and rush to the bathroom and vomit the cheap beer.

John
Present

I wake with a start. My heart is in my throat, and cold sweat saturates my clothing through to my crisp white sheets. I haven't had the dream in a while, months really. But lately, I have been feeling more and more unsettled. With things being so tense between Victoria and I, my anxiety is becoming harder and harder to keep at bay.

We are supposed to be hosting dinner for Victoria's parents this evening, so I try my best to not overthink our relationship. I notice she's already gotten up and is in the kitchen scrubbing the countertop when I walk in, groggy and aching from a restless sleep. She looks up and gives me a wan smile like, she too, had not slept well.

"What are you thinking for the menu tonight?" I ask as I reach for the coffee she'd placed on the island for me.

She sniffs and wipes the sheen of sweat on her forehead with the back of her hand, "We usually do roasted chicken with garlic mashed potatoes and green beans. Sound good?" she smiles.

"Sounds great!" I say, even though I don't really love mashed potatoes. But I am treading lightly, hoping not to create any issues before people arrive.

The phone rings and Victoria's eyes move from the blinking read light of the receiver, to me. "You want to grab that?"

My shoulders stiffen and my head aches at the thought it might be my mother.

"John, you look pale. Are you not feeling well?"

I reassure her with a smile and pick up the phone, "Hello?"

The tightness in my chest dissolves, "Telemarketer," I roll my eyes and take my coffee to the breakfast table. Victoria clucks her tongue and continues cleaning.

When her parents arrive, Vic and her mom move into the kitchen and immediately open a bottle of wine and dive into whatever new gossip there is going around and finish preparing the meal. Marshall and I retreat to my home office. He sits across from me and toys with his glass, the ice clinking against the crystal as he dips it.

Since our last conversation, I committed to a few sessions with a couple's counselor per Victoria's request. I have always had an aversion to therapy but was willing to give it a shot when I saw how much it meant to her. After we had one of our usual arguments involving me not being ready for marriage, I had a sinking feeling that she might pull the plug on us. Instead of helping us, all the session did was flood me with emotions that I didn't want to deal with, and then the whole next day, I felt like a zombie. It was draining, and I can't see that as good for my career. I can't run a successful company if I am on the verge of depression every day. I do have to figure something out though because I know her patience is running thin.

My dream about Rose last night has really thrown me, however. Before I woke, I remember seeing her sitting on the edge of the grass, overlooking the bay. I was standing a generous distance behind her, watching her beautiful hair blowing in the wind. There was a little girl frolicking around behind her, singing a tune I didn't recognize. Neither of them seemed to notice I was there, but there was such a peaceful feeling surrounding the whole scene. I could almost smell the dew on the grass and feel the breeze that whipped her hair. Suddenly, I felt a sick and heavy sensation in the pit of my stomach. I had an urge to retch, and I must have startled them. The little girl stopped singing and ran out of sight and Rose turned to focus on who had interrupted this serene moment for her, but once she saw me, she smiled.

Her smile was just as bright from far away as it was if you were standing right in front of her. The longer she smiled, though, the sicker I felt, and it made me angry. I wanted to enjoy this special moment with Rose. Then, before I knew it, her face changed. I stepped closer clutching my stomach and squinting my eyes...my mother? The little girl raced over and fell into her lap as she stared at me with such intensity that I forgot I was feeling sick. I watched my mother slide the little girl off her lap to play with some wildflowers at her feet. She began to lift an arm as if she wanted me to help her to stand. My sickness quickly turned to rage, and I couldn't control myself. My body flung forward to grab her arm, and I began to yank her violently around. I was sobbing so loudly and thrashing her so violently that when I woke, I thought I might actually vomit with the fury I was feeling.

"So, what are you working on lately?" Marshall asked as he wound his watch, bringing me back to present.

"Oh, you know, we have that new toothpaste ad coming up as well as the new cable company we won over. It's a pretty big deal, so things have just been pretty tense lately," I exhale.

"Maybe you should take some time off? Give yourself a chance to relax?" he suggests. Marshall is always a huge supporter in taking time off. He must have forgotten the struggles of the young professional trying to keep his business afloat in an extremely competitive market.

"I'd love to take a vacation, but there's work to be done and I want to have a good nest egg for us," I smile at the thought of my future with Victoria.

"That's an honorable position to hold, however at this rate, you will eventually wear yourself out," he warned. I reach for the glass of water on the edge of my desk and chug it. I have been parched all day, still unnerved by my dream.

"You're right. I need to find a way to relax," I agree as I lean back in my chair.

"Victoria says you've been having some pretty frequent, vivid dreams?" Marshall raises an eyebrow. I feel so embarrassed. Why would she tell her dad about that?

"Only when I've got a lot going on. It's really nothing though. One too many old-fashioneds before bed, I'm sure," I smile a little too long and hope he doesn't see right through me.

"She said you were yelling out a woman's name," I can feel his eyes piercing into my skull. I don't even know how to explain myself. My heart starts to pound harder, and the sick feeling returns. I excuse myself to the restroom and am relieved to find Marshall has moved to the kitchen when I return. I need a drink. I need to have a serious discussion with Victoria later about oversharing. I appreciate and admire her closeness with her parents, but there were some things she didn't need to tell them, especially when it's about me.

John

I got in my father's car and was consumed by the odor of cigarettes and marijuana residue. The leather seats were cracked and worn, and soda cans littered the floor. My father used to take such care of his car, like he did most things he possessed. He was the polar opposite of my mother, which is likely what drew him to her all those years ago, but while some opposites attract, their particular flavors did not go well together. They created horrors at every turn, like a bad bout of food poisoning.

I rolled the windows down and let the warm breeze air out the car as I drove. New York was still fairly cool out, and I was already growing used to the different climate. There is a soothing nature to the south, however. We may not have the seasons, but we have the quiet, the serenity of being alone. I purposely avoided looking at the Leonards house as I turned away from the neighborhood. I wasn't quite ready to face her. I wasn't ready for any of it, honestly. So, I decided to reacquaint myself. I drove to my high school and was oddly comforted by how nothing had changed. Of course, in just a year's time, it wouldn't have. I had changed, I had become someone altogether different.

Next, I made my way to the old pizza place we used to frequent after practices. It was packed with new faces, but the same staff. I could see their tired faces through the thick-paned glass. I suddenly felt pretty hungry considering I'd just puked the little I did eat earlier in the day and decided to go in for a slice. A bell chimed as I tugged the door open, and my mouth instantly watered at the aroma of fresh garlic bread and melted cheese.

"Heya, John!" Birk, the owner, and pizza-maker extraordinaire waved at me before his face twitched and he followed up with, "So sorry to hear about your dad." I cringed as several faces turned; their expressions sorrowful. "What'll you have? It's on the house." Birk said as he spun a round raw circle of dough in his hands.

"Just a slice of pepperoni, thanks," I smiled and made my way to a table in the far corner. I wish I'd brought a book to have something else to focus on other than the reality that everyone is now pretending not to stare at the guy who is only back in town because his dad died. I should have asked Ben to come along with me instead of leaving him home alone with our mom, but I also didn't like the idea of her being there with dad's body. Who knows what she would have done. In her own demented way, I think she does feel some sadness or remorse now that he's gone. She can't be a total monster.

A waitress quietly set a drink in front of me, "It's Dr. Pepper," she darted her eyes from the drink to me like she's waiting for me to confirm that I did, in fact, want a Dr. Pepper. Which I did. It's the only acceptable drink to have with Birk's pizzas.

I thank her and take a sip, relishing the fizzy sweetness as it hits my tongue.

"John?" a soft voice whispered from my right.

200

I looked up and my heart slammed into my stomach, "Rose! Hey!"

"How have you been?" I can see in her face that I'd hurt her, that she held on to it. The question is a polite courtesy, but her eyes scream I-hate-you-for-abandoning-me.

I shift in my seat to face her, "Okay...just busy with work and school, you know?" Although, she probably didn't know. I'd left without a word. I'd gotten home and couldn't pack my bags and hit the road fast enough. I should have felt ashamed for not trying to go see her, but Roach made it clear, in so many words, that her parents wanted me to stay away. "You look great! I mean...I didn't get to see you before...and I wrote, but I understood you probably didn't want to hear from me."

"You wrote to me?" she sat up straight, skeptical.

"Uh, well yes. I felt terribly that I didn't get to see you in the hospital, but your parents were pissed. I didn't want to be disrespectful and keep trying to go see you when you were recovering. Did you..." I didn't know what to say, or if it was even appropriate to ask how she was after returning home.

"Yeah, they were pretty angry. But that didn't last long," she chuckled. "Almost dying kind of trumped the fact that we lied about the trip. I'm very lucky," she shrugged and smiled. The waitress brought my slice and set it in front of me.

"Yeah, we are all lucky. The whole thing was awful. I am really sorry about all of it...and I have wanted to apologize for leaving without saying goodbye," I leaned in toward her slightly. I'd missed her and didn't realize how much until that moment, seeing her again. "You really look great," I added.

"Yeah, you said that." Her cheeks blushed and she tucked her hair behind her ear. "My mom keeps harassing me, too. Saying how she saved my life, so I better take good care of myself." I must have misheard her.

"Your mom saved your life?"

"Yeah, I lost a lot of blood and she had to donate since they didn't have my blood type in the hospital." The waitress brings her slice and sets it on her table.

"Oh...wow. I'm so glad she could do that. I can't imagine if...you know," I stammer, my pulse is thrumming so hard that I feel a wave of nausea again. "So, otherwise, you've been doing okay?" I ask, but the questions beneath that one roiled under my skin. *Why didn't they give her my letter? What made them that angry at me? Why did her mom lie to her about my donating the blood that saved her?*

A silence fell, and I wasn't sure if she was trying to get back to her meal or if she was waiting for me to say something. I cleared my throat and reached for my pizza that I no longer had an appetite for.

"What brought you back?" she asked just as I took a bite. I turned back to her, and the cheese stretched and slapped molten hot against my chin. I jerked and hurriedly pressed a napkin to my mouth.

"Uh, well my dad died," I said, covering my mouth.

"Oh my gosh! I'm so sorry!" she began, then deflated a bit into her seat. Her fingers playing with the edge of her own pizza slice. It seemed she'd also lost her appetite. "I heard he was sick. Ben missed a lot of school, but I know Eve's mom was on him to finish his work so he wouldn't flunk out," she offered as if I should care. I did care, but I didn't show it well in the last year. "Are you...okay? That's probably a stupid question," she scolded herself and turned slightly away from me.

"I am just glad he's not sick anymore. My family isn't that close," I give a sad smile. "My parents aren't like your parents. I'm sure you've heard stories." She blinked and looked back up at me. Another silence. Another space filled with questions we both weren't going to ask. We ate our pizza in silence for the next few minutes.

"Heya you two..." Birk called from across the restaurant, wiping his hands on his apron. "We're closing up in a few." I looked around and noticed we were only one of two couples in the place now. The other was already standing and collecting their things to leave.

"So..." I said finishing my slice. "Would you want to go somewhere and talk more?"

She sipped the last of her soda and set it on the table, puzzling over the question, likely wondering if I was worth her time. I wasn't, she could have and should have said no after what I'd done, but instead she placed her hands in her lap and grinned, "Sure."

I drop a few bills to cover her meal and we walked together out of the restaurant. The sun still hovered low in the skin, painting it with broad strokes of pink and orange. I guided her to my dad's car, hesitating for a moment. I didn't want her in that car, but I also wasn't ready for the night to end. I wasn't ready to go back to my house and face my mom and Ben. Besides, I would have to spend the next day with them getting Dad's affairs in order, I wasn't going to waste the little time I did have with Rose. But the questions I had kept nagging in the back of my mind.

"Everything okay?" she asked, noticing I had not made a move to open the car door.

"Yeah, just super strange to be back here and seeing you again," I shoved my hands in my pockets. I noticed her expression shift from a nervous smile to a tense apprehension. "I just didn't think you'd talk to me again. I thought you hated me."

She shifted her weight from one foot to the other and crossed her arms, "John, I knew you were going away. I wasn't dumb enough to think a little summer fling was going to keep you here. I just wish you'd said bye," she chewed at her bottom lip and averted her eyes. "Now let's go, I need to get home by 9."

I take her to the only place I knew to go, cheesy as it seemed.

"The pier?" she giggled beside me, and the sound of it took me back to that summer and how ignorant we all were.

I shrugged and turned the car off before getting out and rounding the hood to open her door. "I have nothing but honorable intentions," I bowed and waved my hand for her to exit. She jokingly slapped my shoulder and walked down to the stoned path that lead to the pier.

It was an unusually quiet evening, there was only one other car, but we noticed it was empty. I looked up and down the bank and saw an older man fishing with a young boy. I looked back and Rose was already halfway down the pier. I rushed to catch up, "Where is everyone. I feel like this place used to be packed on a Friday night."

"Things change," she shrugged and kept walking until she reached the end. The wood was old and splintered, but someone left behind a beach towel, so we spread it across the edge and slipped our shoes off. I helped her to sit and she swung her legs over to dip her toes in the water. She squeaked at the chill, then allowed them to lower deep enough to go halfway up her calves. I bent and rolled my jeans up and did the same.

"So, you're liking it in New York?" she spoke first. A safe question.

I nodded, "I do, actually. It's so different, and I think I needed that. Things at my house were so stressful. I felt like I was suffocating."

"Hmm," she bobbed her head, "I know the feeling all too well."

"How is your senior year?" I asked. "And why were you alone on a Friday night?"

I watched as she kicked her feet lightly in the water. Her toes were painted a soft pink that matched the sunset. "It's going well, but if I thought my parents were over protective before, it's like hyperdrive now. They made me quit cheer because they were afraid I was too weak. I'm fully recovered now, but what's the point? I graduate in a month."

"Where are you going to school?" I asked.

"Well, they think I'm going to get my basics here at the community college. But I applied to Brown and got in. I'm waiting for the right time to tell them. That's kind of why I was at Birk's tonight. I needed a minute," she took a band from her wrist and began tying her long blonde hair up into a knot on top of her head.

Brown is not far from me.

"I did write to you," I said, unsure if it mattered anymore.

"Well, I didn't get it. Like I said, ultra strict parents."

"I'm s--"

"John, stop apologizing. It was a summer trip. I knew the rules. You needed to escape and you did." I tensed at her words. As much as she claimed not to be upset, it's clear she still held some resentment.

"I needed to escape here, not *you*. I wrote the letter so you'd know that. I was trying to see if there was a chance for us to...I dunno, keep in touch until you graduated," I spoke quickly so she wouldn't cut me off.

She considered my words, folding her legs underneath her to warm her feet. "I kept having this dream after the accident."

"Yeah?"

"Not as often now, but for weeks I would be back in that hospital bed, feeling so tired and trying to talk, but my throat kept closing up. And then my mom would be crying to the doctor, screaming at him to help me because she couldn't, that he wasn't doing his job. Which, you know, very typical mom, but then my dad kept saying *test the boy*. Just weird. I know dreams are like, a way for your body to work out stress, but it felt so real."

Of course, the boy in her dream, is me.

"I know it was you," she interrupted my thoughts, and for a second I thought I'd spoken them out loud. "I know

206

you saved my life." Tears welled in her eyes and spilled over her cheeks.

"It wasn't just a summer fling to me. At least, I didn't think of you that way." I wanted to reach over and hold her, comfort her, but it felt like such a fragile moment.

"My mother wedges herself in every part of my life. School, activities, friendships. It's like she lives vicariously through me and obsesses over me. I don't feel like I'm living my own life. She even lied about saving me to maintain control over me! God forbid I have a connection with anyone else more than I do with her," she choked on her words and buried her face in her hands.

I couldn't help myself. I scooted closer and wrapped my arm around her thin, vulnerable frame. "I get that. I really do."

She pulled back and looked up at me. I could feel her heart pounding in her chest against mine, but all I could do was remember that I'd told her I would be a gentleman. I am leaving in 2 days. She will be going to Brown. She deserved to start her adult life on her own terms the same way I had been able to. I felt her hand twine through my arm. She pinched lightly at the skin on my knuckles then ran the tips of her fingers along the length of mine. "You saved my life. Brown isn't that far from NYU," she spoke softly.

I swallowed, understanding the meaning behind what she'd said. I heard a car door shut in the distance, and I think of the man and his son packing up their tackle box, hoping they'd caught something.

Rose looked up at me and in that moment, I had hope that maybe that wouldn't be the last time I saw her. That she was choosing to see me because she wanted to and not because it was what I wanted. I leaned in slightly and watched her run her tongue along her bottom lip. For the first time, I was happy to be back. But it didn't last long, because just as I allowed myself to think it, I heard her voice.

"John? What in the hell are you doing here with *her*?"

My mother has arrived.

John

"What are you doing here?" I asked over my shoulder. Rose's eyes widen at my cold voice.

"I went out looking for you. We were hoping to have a nice family dinner considering we are all in town," she took slow, deliberate steps toward us and I became more rigid the closer she got. "Should have known you would want to run off and find *her*."

Rose and I stood up, cornered and wondering which version of my mother we were going to receive. Well, I was wondering, Rose was looking at a woman she'd only heard of through the town gossip. Like folklore passed down over generations. I hadn't spoken to my mother since the hospital, and I can't say that I'd missed her. In the year away, I'd felt calmer than I had in my entire life and just being near her again drudged up the ghosts of old wounds. I'd taken a psychology class in my second semester and learned about childhood trauma and how it effects you even if you couldn't remember what happened. It's in you, forever.

I turn to address Rose, "I'll take you home." She nods and smiles, crossing her arms nervously over her chest as if she'd been caught doing something wrong.

"Weren't you going to introduce us, John?" My mother planted her feet 10-feet from us. Her eyes twinkled in the way they always did when she was teetering on the edge. I rolled my eyes and didn't reply, rather just held Rose's hand and tugged her down to pass my mother so we could get to the car. "I guess we don't really need an introduction, though, do we?" she called after us, snark laced in her voice.

"Just ignore her," I instructed. We were 25 feet from the car and the sun was slipping quickly down below the tree line. Rose didn't speak, but I heard her quick and shallow breaths as she hurried along.

"Don't you want to know why?" Her voice felt as though she was only steps behind us, like her voice was the wind itself.

I still didn't respond. I knew better than to engage her. We were 10 feet from the car.

"What does she mean?" Rose whispered beside me.

"No idea," I replied because I didn't. I heard her feet leave the wood of the pier and began shuffling through the grass. I turned back briefly; she was still calmly following behind. It was unnerving how serene she appeared because she did nothing without purpose. Even if it made no sense to anyone else, my mother did everything with focused intention.

"You have such pretty hair, Rose. Interesting how you have such beautiful blonde hair while your parents don't." I sighed heavily and felt dizzy with rage.

"Go back home and leave her alone!" I growled toward her, but I had to admit that I was curious what she was getting at.

We reached the car. I fumbled for the keys and shoved it in the door so I could quickly open it for Rose to get in. Just as I got it open and stepped back to allow Rose space to get in, she hit us with a boulder.

"I had that same, shiny blonde hair when I was your age. Of course, it's dull now, like everything else when you get older. But I must say, it's like looking into a mirror of the past with you," she was close then, arms reach. Rose's face blanched and she looked like she was about to be sick.

"What the hell are you talking about?" I turned to face her; the act alone felt like I'd opened a door that I never should have. One that was never meant to be opened and one that would never be closed.

"I knew they would never tell you." My mother threw her head back, exasperated. "I tried at the hospital, because of course your father hid it from me, too. He controlled everything, you know?" she placed her hands on her hips and pursed her lips. "Rick never seemed that intimidating. He was always such a wisp of a man, a spineless...well, I guess I shouldn't speak ill of the dead. He was your father, after all. But he did have a way about him that got people to trust him. Like a sneaky snake..."

"What. Are. You. Saying?" I ground out through my teeth. I shouldn't have asked, I should have just shut the door and got in and drove away. But I was frozen. I hated my mother; in that moment it was confirmed. Still, I wanted to hear what she was about to say. Something bigger than me held me there, forcing me to listen because even though I hated her, she was about to reveal something huge, something important. Something devastating.

"I am Rose's mother," she let the words fall over us.

"Oh my God," Rose crumpled inward, curling into a ball. "What is she saying?" she added, looking up briefly, her face twisted and anguished.

"How?" the word released from my mouth without any encouragement.

"I was pregnant with her during a very dark time." My mother's shoulders sagged as if relieved to finally say it out loud. "Your father found out I had an affair, and after I'd had a little mishap with you, he put me in the crazy house. He told me that I miscarried, that my fit had caused us to lose our child. He *blamed* me for her death!" Tears spilled from her eyes and her words became rounded with a renewed sense of agony.

"For all that time, I thought I'd lost my baby. My baby girl that I'd always wanted, and when I finally got her, he...he took her away," she coughed out a sob and tilted her head at Rose, taking her in. She did favor her. And just as I began connecting the dots, there was something in the recesses of my mind that told me it was true. I couldn't have been much more than a year old when it happened, long before I was able to preserve any memories, but I knew it was true. My body sagged against the car as she continued.

"Those people had the audacity to allow you to save her without telling you why it had to be you. They lied to you, they lied to her, Rick lied to all of us!" she laughed now, a pitchy, wild cackle. "And I'm the crazy one! Isn't that funny?!" she bent over, wrapping her arms around her waist, and laughed.

"Take me home. Please," Rose spoke softly from within the car. I suddenly felt filthy. I didn't want to be anywhere near her, and not because she was my half-sister

212

that I was very close to doing things with that would be considered illegal in most states, but because just like I predicted, I ruined her because I had been ruined. My mother ruined everything.

I eyed her for a few seconds, watching as she stood there simultaneously crying and laughing, likely feeling a strong sense of validation for herself, but I had no sympathy. I didn't want to comfort my mother at all. I wanted to get away from her, away from here. Away from the lies and torment and shit. But I had to stay until the funeral. I owed it to Ben. I closed Rose's door and edged my way to the driver's side, "You stay away from the house. I better not see you at dad's funeral," I shouted, my words chipped and broken. I didn't give her a chance to respond.

It was dark by the time I threw the car in reverse; the sun was only a faint glow along the horizon as I pulled away in silence. I thought I saw Roach's truck parked on the farther side of the clearing, but I couldn't focus long enough to be sure. The only thing I could think about was that Rose was sitting beside me. Rose. The girl that I thought I had a special connection with in all the ways you'd want to with your first love but turns out it was because she was my sister.

My fucking sister.

And everyone knew but us.

John
Present

Marshall is talking but his voice sounds like he's speaking to me while I'm under water. He's asking me questions, but I can't quite make out what he's saying. My body is becoming rigid and my fists clench into tight balls as I dig them into my seat cushion. My head thrashes side to side, and the more I try to contain myself, the more powerless I am. I can't stop what's happening, and I don't understand why my body is betraying me. One minute I was completely fine and the next thing I know, every part of me feels detached and running independently as if I had short circuited and nobody could find the breaker box.

"Help!" I plead. Beads of sweat trickle down my face and drip like little shocks of electricity onto my chest and neck. My skin is burning. I want to rip my shirt off to cool down, but I can't move.

"Just try to calm down John, try to get through it. You must get through this part to heal. Keep pushing through," Marshall directs. All I can think is, I must be having a seizure if nobody is willing to touch me.

"Breathe, John. Take deep breaths and continue," Marshall says sternly as he locks eyes with me. Then, suddenly, the phone rings.

"Don't answer!" I scream.

"John, I think you need to answer it. I think it's time you calm down and just answer the phone." Marshall presses. I'm still disoriented, but I force myself to breathe as Marshall instructed and little by little I begin to relax.

"Get Victoria. I want her to be here," I demand. But as my eyes allow me to focus on Marshall, he shakes his head.

"You can do this on your own. Just answer the phone, John." I bury my head in my hands.

"I can't do it. I can't." I wipe my brow with a handkerchief and dab the back of my neck.

"It's time. You can do this John. Keep going." I look at him, sitting across from me and watch him calmly clasp his hands into his lap. I reach over and pick up the receiver.

John

Rose was still curled in a tight ball beside me, whimpering and dabbing her eyes with the sleeve of her sweater. I didn't know what to say to her, how to explain that this feeling she was having was grossly normal for me. I expected nothing less from my family, but hers was now completely turned upside-down, and she now carried the burden of having to confront her own mother. Or I guess the woman who had played the role of her mother for her whole life. Was she ever going to tell her that she was adopted? Surely, the scare at the hospital had threatened to blow the roof off of their happy home, but mothers tend to be good at lying to their children.

Santa.

The tooth fairy.

Unconditional love.

Why not this?

"Just so you know, I really had no idea," it was probably the dumbest thing to say, but I honestly had no clue what to tell her. "I'm sorry that's how you had to find out."

Rose didn't speak for a while. She stared out at the road, but I could hear the questions swimming in her head. Birk's pizza place came into view, and I knew this would be the last time we saw each other and was both relieved and deeply saddened. As I pulled up into the empty parking lot, aside from Rose's car, she turned slightly, but stiffly toward me, "I'm sorry, too. I'm still in shock, but it makes sense, doesn't it? I never felt like, connected to my parents like I saw other kids were. I always thought it was because she was so overprotective but turns out it's because she was keeping this secret from me my whole life."

I laughed cynically, "What are you going to say to your parents?"

She chewed her thumbnail and shook her head back and forth, back and forth, "I guess I just have to be straightforward, you know?" she scoffed, "It actually is perfect, because now I can tell them I'm going away to college, and they can't say a damn thing about it."

College. That conversation seemed like an eternity ago. The idea that she was going to be only a few hours from where I was gone from feeling hopeful, to painful.

"Word of advice?" I shifted into park and turned to face her. She waited for me to continue, and I winced at how distraught she looked, how destroyed she was because of my mother. Because of me. "Don't be so hard on them. You wouldn't have wanted Patrice as a mother."

"I can't wait to get the hell out of here," she said before opening the car door and getting out. I expected her to get in her own car and take off, wanting nothing to do with me, but she paused and twisted back around to face me. "This isn't your fault, John. Don't let her hurt you anymore. I know I won't. We are in control now."

I swallowed; my throat too tight to have spoken even if I had words to say. I lifted my hand, offering a wave goodbye. She gave me the saddest smile before getting into her car and pulling out of the parking lot. I didn't want to go back to the house, but I also didn't know where else to go. I slammed my fists into the steering wheel causing the horn to honk loud and echo into the night. I screamed obscenities and heaved, feeling like vomiting again or crying or punching someone in the face. I needed air, so I threw the door open and began pacing the parking lot. My shoes crunching on gravel, kicking at an empty soda cup that someone didn't have the decency to throw away. I heard wheels scraping as they turned into the lot, and so help me if my mother followed me here...but, it wasn't her. I saw Roach through the rolled down windows, country music was blaring as he drove up beside me, his face sullen as he turned his truck off and waited.

"You knew, didn't you." I felt feral, spit flew from my mouth.

I watched as he opened his door, cautiously as if entering a lion's den.

"Who else? Mickey? Jen? Mary Beth? Did everyone fucking know she was my sister?!" I screamed and fisted my hands, pacing again.

"They didn't know. They still don't. This is on me, okay man? I'm sorry," he came to me and tried placing a hand on my shoulder, but I slapped it off. Then I took both my hands and shoved him as hard as I could.

"You're my best friend! My brother! And you are just like them, aren't you?!" I shoved him again, and watched as he averted his gaze and let me. "What? What else?"

His lip twitched, but he didn't speak.

"Why were you at the pier? That was you, wasn't it? Why were you there?" More pieces started to come together.

My mother couldn't have walked from the house. He'd brought her there. It's where he brought all his girls.

"You-you're fucking sick. You two deserve each other." I suddenly felt tired and weak. "She's not at the house, is she?"

Roach sucked in a breath, then shook his head no.

"Good. I don't want to see her. Make sure she stays the fuck away from my dad's funeral," I paced back to the car and heard him clear his throat from right behind me.

"I'm so--" he began and before I could think twice, I whirled around and slammed my fist into his jaw.

"And that goes for you, too.

Back at the house, I could see the living room light was on. Not the one in my father's bedroom, nor the room Ben and I shared. Both of those windows had the curtains drawn. It looked abandoned. I didn't really take a look around when Ben first brought me back, and it could have just look more pathetic in the cloak of night, maybe it always appeared that way. I just didn't realize when I was living in it. Like when people have a bad house smell, but don't realize it. The front flowerbed was full of dead bushes, uneven twigs jutted out here and there. The mulch was now just dried, impacted chips. The grass was overgrown in some areas, mostly with weeds.

"We're out back!" Ben's voice called from the backyard. "Becky, not mom," he added, and I wondered if she'd already reported back that big bad John yelled at her. I was so angry, the last thing I wanted to do was face another person who might have been part of this monumental lie, but I reminded myself I was only here for one more day.

219

One more day and I could go back to New York where there were hundreds of other people with way more fucked up lives than mine.

I followed the smell of marijuana and was surprised to find Becky finishing an inhale before passing the blunt to Ben. She noticed the look of shock on my face, and I noticed the fine lines on hers. Becky had aged like a movie star. Her hair was still in a sleek bob, but it was grey. Not the kind of wiry, dusty color some people are unfortunate enough to have, but a glossy silver almost that made her sparkle in the moonlight.

"Where's Eve?" I asked.

"At a girlfriend's house. Teenagers never want to hang out with their moms," she ran a polished finger through her hair and stood to meet me. "It's so good to see you, John." She smelled of that fancy perfume she's worn for as long as I could remember.

"Good to see you, too." I was a full foot taller than she was, and my chin could rest comfortably on her head.

"Come," she said, wrapping her thin hands around mine and guiding me to an empty chair beside her. Ben offered me the blunt, and I took it gladly. I was never really into recreational drugs after having watch my mother succumb to them so tragically over the years, but I was so wound up and my knuckles hurt from punching Roach. We sat there, listening to the rattle of the cicadas and croaking frogs, a southern symphony, and another thing that you'll never hear in the busy city I now call home.

"I'll put the house on the market next Monday. I have a cleaning crew coming day after tomorrow, and an estate sale by the end of the week. You're welcome to go through the house and take what you like. I'll split everything down the middle and send you each a check. Your father had a sizable life insurance policy that will be direct deposited in your accounts," Becky listed it all off in that organized way of hers.

"Thank you for handling everything," I said, and I meant it. I wanted nothing to do with that house or anything in it.

"I'm moving to California," Ben spoke from beside me, reaching for the blunt.

"What are you going to do there?" I asked, feeling guilty that I hadn't known his plans, that I talked to him so rarely and never about his personal life.

"Dad emancipated me, and I found a job there. Just need a fresh start."

"Wow...you sure you're ready to go out on your own?" I asked, my face grew hot when he gave me a look that said why-do-you-give-a-shit-all-of-a-sudden?

"I'm going with my boyfriend," he said, flatly. Becky huffed out a giggle.

"Ben is moving across the country with that boy, the carrot top. You remember him?" Becky pointed at me, her smile wide. I would have never pegged her to be so open-minded, but she was also high as a kite.

"Wesley?" I looked to Ben. "You and he are a thing?"

He nodded, a hint of what looked like contentment on his face, "Yup. He graduated early, wants to be an actor," Ben rolled his eyes.

"Where is she," I asked, changing subjects mostly to be sure I didn't have to stress about her.

"At a hotel," Becky chimed in, her tone firm and protective as it always had been.

"Did you know?" I looked at each of them.

Ben nodded.

"Rose is Ted's daughter," Becky grabbed the blunt and took a long inhale then blew it into the air above her.

I didn't know what I expected her to say, but that definitely wasn't it.

John

"Why didn't anyone tell me?" It's the question I kept asking myself and I needed someone, anyone to answer it.

Ben shrugged and leaned his elbows on his knees, "I didn't know you were trying to screw the girl. At the time, I was worried I'd almost lost my brother, then I was taking care of Dad, and then you left."

"Even if you didn't know about me and Rose, you knew we had a sister, a half sister, and didn't tell me."

"Tell you and what? You'd decide to come home? Start having family dinners with your fag brother and sister you had the hots for like one big happy family?"

"Language!" Becky choked out.

"I didn't do anything with her!" I didn't know why I was defending myself, but I think I felt more of a pull to defend Rose's honor. A rumor like that would be devastating. I wondered if she'd confronted her parents when she got home, or had her mother found some way to brush it off, call us a bunch of liars. She was clearly a very convincing woman. "How long did you know?" I turned to Becky who was staring out across the yard.

"I'd always had a feeling she'd not been faithful to your father. I'd considered each of you being...not Rick's, but apparently, he'd done a paternity test on Ben and was very certain that you were his. You were conceived...intentionally, and before she became...what she is." Becky spoke as if she'd had a very long time to digest it all. Which, in essence, she did. She spent so much time with my mother over the years, understanding her likely in a way that even my dad hadn't.

"But how did you know it was Ted's?" Ben asked.

She took another inhale and smiled as she blew it through her lips. "Because your father wrote to him after her stay at the mental facility. Basically, a back-off-or-else type of thing. I found it when I was going through the closet to find baby blankets."

Ben didn't appear shocked, but I felt like I'd been physically shoved back in my seat, "Wait...why were you looking for baby blankets? When was this?"

"Oh, a month or so before you graduated. A happy surprise!" she smiled, and it looked to reach every good part of her. Becky was a wonderful mother. "He's a little over a year now. I have a nanny since, you know, I kicked Ted out."

"Where's Ted now?" I asked because I truly had no other words. My mother had effectively destroyed the only people in her life that ever cared for her. And for what? Did it weigh on her conscience at all?

"Not far. Of course, he wants 50/50 custody now that he has a son. He showed so little care for Eve in those early years, but now he gives a damn. Imagine that," she humphs and sits back in her seat.

"What did the letter say?" Ben asked. I was curious, too. I knew so little of what made my father tick, what might cause him distress as I never witnessed him angry or frustrated, or anything other than a mild-mannered sap.

She wordlessly reached beside her, into her purse and slipped out an envelope. "I keep it. I know that seems ridiculous, but it's a reminder that I will never go back to that life."

I never thought much about Becky's personal life, outside of the fact that it was perfect. That Ted was perfect, Eve was perfect, and Becky kept their home neat, tidy and smelling of fresh baked delicacies every single day. It never occurred to me that she might have been unhappy. That Ted wasn't a perfect husband. My father had to have been unhappy too, but never showed it either. Is that what it's like being an adult? Do they all mask how much they wish they had it differently? Is every marriage doomed? I can't imagine living another day being miserable because of someone else, and they stayed stuck for years.

Ben reached and took the paper from her outstretched hand and held it between us to read together:

Ted

I understand we all have our flaws. I know that in life there is no perfect person, and we all have to find ways to accept one another as it is the courteous thing to do. What is also courteous, however, is for a man to not take advantage of a sick woman and a good friend. A Christian man to not covet his neighbor's wife. As I sit watching my wife deteriorate before my eyes, I have to be the one to decide how to care for her. How to care for the baby inside of her. The baby that I know is not mine. The baby that I know is yours. She has asked for you several times as she is out of her mind and unaware of where she is or who I am. You had your fun and now I am the one left to clean up the mess you two have made. I think of myself as a level-headed man, a respectful man but what I cannot bring myself to do, is raise a child that does not belong to me. I take it this is not something you wish your wife to be privy to, so I have decided to send the child off to be adopted by a loving family who is in no way connected to this shameless situation. I want to make it clear that you are under no circumstance to come near my wife again. Consider this the last favor you will ever receive from me.

    Regards,

    Rick

"Wow, he was really pissed. Very *may I speak to your manager* but like, with adultery," Ben chuckled and handed the letter back.

"Do you think he was only doing that with my mom?" I asked.

Becky shrugged, "He tried to deny it was even true, saying they were crazy, and we always knew it, so why believe this...but, with the letter was a copy of the adoption papers, so I found the date of birth, did the math...there was a solid month he claimed to be working late on some project at the office. That also happened to be a time where Patrice was often leaving the house, leaving *you*. It just made sense. A woman knows, and I've seen the girl around. She does favor Patrice, but there's so much of Ted in her mannerisms, her chin has the same dimple. It doesn't matter if it were one time or twenty, he had a child with someone else and allowed me to cater to her like some sister wife. It's sick. It's just sick."

226

"I'm surprised they didn't move away the second they found out. Clearly, her mom did not want Rose to find out," my shoulders were tensing so much that I ached.

"Well, you left. Your father wasn't about to do anything, he wanted nothing to do with her from the start. That only left us," Becky waved her hand in the air. "And Ted wasn't about to tarnish his own image by entertaining this lovechild of his and the crazy woman across the street. Best Rose finish school here. She didn't know any different. Another secret. Another tether to your family," Becky sighed. I wondered how often she'd cursed herself for ever being friends with my mother, how different her life might have been if she'd never gotten close to our family.

"Will you come tomorrow?" Ben asked her.

"Of course. In a lot of ways, Rick and I relied on each other through so much and didn't need to talk about it. I loved you boys so much, as if you were my own. Ha! I guess I am her sister wife..." she smiled again, but this time it was sadder, like reflecting on what a shit hand we all were dealt and survived it anyway. "Of course, I will come pay my respects to Rick."

John

I could hardly sleep that night despite how exhausted I was. My bones ached with want of a good night's rest, but my mind raced with all the things that happened in order for us to be here. I thought about Becky and what a dedicated wife and mother she'd always been, how she was there for Ben and I when she didn't need to be and had so little to show for it. Her husband had betrayed her, just as my mother had betrayed my father. I thought back to that time as a child when I'd watched my mother in her bedroom, crying into my father's stiff shoulders as he walked away from her and realized that it wasn't my father after all. It had been Ted all along. Ted and my mother had created Rose, and my father...my father who bent over backwards to keep our family together, had tossed her aside. I could not wrap my head around it. I could not picture my father being so cold and casting away a child like that. I guess everyone has a limit.

I thought about Ben and wondered how he would fare in California. I felt shameful for not being a better brother to him, for being selfish and leaving without making sure he was okay. Looking back, I acted as my mother always had. I left when I was overwhelmed.

I thought about Roach and how it didn't feel as good as I hoped when I punched him. He didn't follow me home and the phone did not ring. I pictured him with my mom in some seedy hotel and clenched my teeth at the idea that he was consoling her. She did not deserve it, I didn't care what she said about what happened back then, she still had an affair. She still did things that I have no recollection of, but the scars remain. Can you understand what it's like to feel panic about things and have no idea why?

The attacks started as soon as I'd left, and I could not find rhyme or reason for them. I walked into a grocery store to get things for my dorm, and a cashier called a manager on the intercom which caused my heart to race, my head thrummed between my ears. It was an immense pressure that almost brought me to my knees if there hadn't been a bench right beside me. I hated taking baths, only showers, ever. I hate hearing Elvis Presley and when he died, it's all they played on the radio. I stopped listening to the radio.

I thought of Rose and was sickened by what almost happened between us. How much worse things would have been if we had done what we clearly were both wanting to do. What would she do now and how would this news affect her?

I checked my watch in the sliver of moonlight as Ben snored beside me, both of us unwilling to sleep in our mother's room. It had always been a forbidden place to us.

4:03 am

"You gonna go see Rose again, aren't you," Ben's voice cracked through the shadows.

"I thought you were sleeping," I whisper, but there's no need.

"You won't stop moving and creaking the damn springs."

"I punched Roach." I feel bad about it. The more I think about it, the more it weighs on me. "I should go apologize."

Ben barks out a laugh, "Roach is an asshole. When are you going to wake up and realize that?"

"Roach is an idiot, not an asshole," I correct.

"No, John. He's been screwing mom for years behind your back. He paid for dad's care because he felt guilty, not because he cares about you."

I swallow and take a deep breath. I don't know if I can forgive Roach for being with my mom behind my back. I've been lied to so much in my life and trusted him and Mickey so intensely, I never imagined he would be one of the ones to have betrayed me. But I should at least hear him out. I know how my mother can be when she sets her fangs into someone.

"So, are you going to go talk to Rose?"

"There's nothing left to say. Besides, we have to go finalize everything at the funeral home before the services today."

"Nobody's gonna come, man. It'll just be us. Not one person visited since you left, only Becky. They let da-" his voice broke, and he cleared his throat before continuing, "They let him rot here like he was trash. He deserved better."

"We'll be there."

Ben scoffed at my reply and turned over. "Yep, and you can run back to New York before they shovel the last bit of dirt on him."

"That's not fair. You're moving away," I lift myself onto my shoulder, but he doesn't face me.

"Dad's dead, John. I was here, watching him die while you ran off and lived it up. You know what's not fair? Changing your dad's sheets because he shits himself four nights in a row. Or staying up all night making sure he doesn't choke and die on his own vomit. Or fending mom off when she randomly decided to show up with whatever guy was dumb enough to get trapped in her web and wanted money. I'm barely 16, John. You didn't think I needed you? I wasn't about to have Becky come deal with this, she'd done enough and has her own kids. We needed *you*!"

I sat up and swung my legs over the edge of the bed, "I'm sorry, Ben."

"Yeah, well, it's not just me you needed to apologize to, but too late now. You're too late."

I lay awake until the sun peeked through the screen of our window. It was almost 7:00 am at that point, in a few hours I would be gone again and this time, for good. The panic threatened to rise again, my fists clenched my ratty bedsheets and I inhaled, counting to 10 and exhaled. Ben was right. I was a terrible son, a terrible brother, and he'd be better off when I was gone.

I just wish I'd said more to make things right with my brother that day.

John

The day of my father's funeral is a blur. Ben didn't say much to me as we got dressed and scoured the pantry and refrigerator for something that could pass as breakfast. I turned at the sound of rustling plastic and found him unwrapping a basket of fruits and pastries on the table.

"Becky," we said in unison.

We ate through the contents in silence. The house already felt different. It looked exactly the same for the most part, but everything that tied memories to it, were not there. I didn't smell my mother's perfume mixed with nicotine. I didn't smell remnants of whatever my father had cooked and placed in carefully portioned Tupperware containers. There were pill bottles lined along the small bar area and a walker beside my father's recliner. A pair of bifocals perched atop a word search that was sitting on the TV tray on the other side. That's what my father boiled down to. He worked, he came home, he cooked, he sat. Day after day, year after year, because after my mother had her way with him, there was very little left of him to amount to anything else.

I looked over to the hallway when Ben spoke, "They took him while you were out yesterday. Roger stayed up late to have him ready for today." I felt a pang of guilt at the rush of it all, the lack of honor and respect for my father.

But he wasn't a man who wanted all kinds of attention and would likely have requested it be just as it was going. A slow, quiet slip into the afterlife. No muss, no fuss.

I nodded as my eyes landed on his closed door. "We should get going." I wiped my mouth on a paper napkin that was also provided by Becky in the basket. Ben didn't reply, rather just scooted his chair back, and placed our dishes in the sink. Today would be my last day in this house, in this town. By next week, next month, it would house another family and hopefully hold far better memories than we'd given it over the years.

"Wesley just pulled up. He offered to drive us over," Ben shrugged a nice-looking tailored jacket over his thin frame.

As we walked toward the front door, I paused and turned to face him, "I hope you know that I was never...that I didn't mean to be a bad brother," I tried, but Ben lifted a hand, waving away my words.

"Not doing this now. Today is about Dad. We can hash it out after," Ben shook his head and swung the door open. Immediately, I noticed his shoulders relax significantly, a broad grin spread across his face as he opened his arms toward the waiting vehicle, toward Wesley.

"Your chariot awaits!" Wesley yelled in a British accent through the open window. I envied the comfort and warmth that flowed between them. In my time away, I had not made any attempt to be close to anyone, romantically nor platonically. I wanted to go to class, go to work, to prove...what? I still wasn't sure. But I did know that relationships made things complicated, and I didn't want complicated. Returning for just a day had reminded me of that. My mind went to Rose again. I couldn't wait to board my plane back to New York.

"Hey, John," Wesley craned his neck to me once I lowered myself into the backseat of his sedan. "Good to see you...sad this is the reason for your visit, but I just went up there and he really looks good. Roger did a great job on him," he smiled and dipped his chin.

"You went to the funeral home?" I asked.

"He works at the flower shop, did all the arrangements for free," Ben gave Wesley a longing look, one that is saved for lovers, and patted his knee as Wesley pulled out onto the road.

"Least I could do. Your dad was beyond kind to me this past year," Wesley gripped the wheel and I noticed his neck flush like Mickey's used to do.

"What did he do?" I asked, unsure if I was prying or not.

"My parents ahh...well they kicked me out when they found out about Ben and me. I had nowhere to go and your dad offered me to stay, no strings attached. It's how I was able to save up so much for this move."

"Wow, that's cool of him," I said. I never thought of my father as being so open-minded. Yet another thing I'd failed to appreciate about him. Of course, he'd be kind enough to lend his home. Just not to his wife's bastard child, I guess.

The rest of the ride, Ben and Wesley discussed details of their move, timing and who was to pack what. Ben was getting Dad's car, which was fine with me, besides, he would need it more than I would. They seemed to genuinely care for one another, and thinking back on Ben just a few years ago, it was good to know he had someone who would have his back.

A few minutes later, we pulled into the parking lot of the funeral home. I'd never been to one and likely passed this building a hundred times in my life and never thought twice of it. Now, it felt like a museum of the dead. A chill ran down my spine at the thought of how many dead people were laid to rest on these grounds, how many people's loved ones had met their maker under a multitude of circumstances. I shivered and something within me felt a physical rejection with each step closer to their doors. But, I was here for my father, for Ben, so I kept on. My feet felt leaden as Wesley held the door open patiently and still sporting that sympathetic smile with a glassy-eyed stare. I couldn't help the eye roll that I gave as I walked past him. He barely knew my dad; how could he possibly feel so strongly for a man he'd only known for a year. Hell, I knew him my entire life and struggled to feel what most sons would at a time like this.

We made our way to the funeral director's office and found a comically short, round man with only a tuft of straggly hair sprouting from just above his forehead. "I'm Roger!" he spoke directly to me, emphasizing how little I've contributed to my father's last moments above ground. "Your father is in the Blue Room, as from his records that's what he wanted, and ah, let's see--" he tuts as he scans whatever document he's holding.

"Why the Blue Room?" I asked, not that it mattered, but I was curious.

"Oh! Well, I guess that's because it's the same room that his parents were viewed in as well. People get very sentimental with these things," he smiled over the stack of papers in his hands. His belly was pushing through his white shirt, the buttons holding on for dear life with spots of perspiration dotting in random places. "He's in the suit you provided Nancy, the box is also tucked nicely beside him--I made certain--and I believe we are squared away on cost. So, if you will just sign down here, we can open the doors!" Roger placed the papers on the desk and directed Ben, not me, to sign along a line that was highlighted.

"What's in the box?" I asked, looking to each of them now. Roger clamped his lips shut and clasped his hands across his girth.

Ben signed the papers and shrugged, "Not sure. I didn't ask. He just wanted it to be buried with him."

Roger escorted us to the Blue Room and unlocked the doors. As he pulled them open, we were hit with the overwhelmed scent of flowers. I was taken aback by the sight of the room. Yes, the walls were blue, hence the name I guess, but all along the wall behind the casket was floor-to-ceiling flowers. Not just your typical bouquets of roses or those weird ones that look like odd-shaped cups, but vibrant bunches of every color spread from wall to wall in the most beautiful display I'd ever seen.

"You did this?" I looked to Wesley who beamed bright pink beside me.

"I did! I have a thing about flowers," he replied, walking into the room, and adjusting petals here and there before moving to my father's coffin and gazing in. He whispered something I couldn't make out before turning to us, waiting.

236

I hadn't really thought about that moment up until we were there, seeing my father for the last time and what that would feel like. Ben strode ahead of me, placed his hand on Wesley's shoulder and leaned into him. Another intimate moment that I didn't feel I should be a part of, I didn't belong here, but I continued forward and stood on the other side of my brother. My chest felt tight as I looked at my father. Not because he looked sickly, not even because he was dead, but in fact looked peaceful as if he were in a comfortable sleep. Like he was dreaming of something pleasant. Ben choked on a sob and Wesley wrapped an arm across his shoulders and guided him to a velvet cushioned seat. There were six rows of 8 chairs each, and I wondered if anything, but the front row would be occupied.

I remained, taking in the details of him. How well they made him look, how neatly they'd dressed him and manicured his nails. His watch shined like new on his wrist. Then, my eyes caught on the box Roger had mentioned. I couldn't help myself, so I reached in and lifted the lid.

Photos. Photos of, what I assume, was him as a child, in the arms of his parents. Both grinning with pride as they held their baby between them. I'd never met my grandparents, and he'd never spoken of them. Yet, he wanted this particular photo to be buried with him for eternity. I slid it over and there were more from his childhood, then one of him and my mother on their wedding day looking so young and happy. Then there's one of my mother holding me, and I only know it's me because of the hair, Ben's was always very bright blonde. I'd never seen any of these pictures. I didn't even know my parents owned a camera.

"Hey, John," a soft, feminine voice whispered from behind me.

John

I turned to face her, "Eve? You came!" I noticed Ben looked up sharply, his eyes narrowed on her back before he turned back to continue whatever conversation he was having. She stammered a bit, picked at her fingers and before she spoke. I noticed Becky ushering in her little boy through the doorway. She's a beautiful girl, I imagined she looked like Becky did at that age. Becky caught my eyes and gave a slight wave before making her way over to Ben and Wesley to pay her respects.

"Of course, I did," Eve puffed out air, likely feeling awkward talking to me after all this time. "I guess I wanted to make sure to say bye. You kind of left and we didn't really see each other. It was abrupt," she looked hurt, her eyebrows pinched together. Her gaze wandered past me to my father and frowned. "He looks good," her voice was light and hopeful. A fresh feeling of self-loathing came over me. I'd been raised with Eve like a sudo-sister, and she was right. I'd left her and Becky without a proper goodbye.

"I'm sorry to hear about your parents," I pictured Ted at some sticky bar, hitting on women far too young for him, thinking he still had the same chiseled looks he'd maintained in his youth. But surely by now, he was succumbing to age like most middle-aged men do. He and my mother had crossed a pretty solid boundary, but I wasn't as much disgusted by them for myself and Ben, we had never known healthy boundaries. But Eve?

Eve sighed, her eyes brimmed with tears, "Yeah, it was a weird year. Luckily, I had Ben, and Rose and I have gotten close. I'm so glad she recovered well after the accident. Oddly, it kind of bonded us."

If only she knew.

And just as the thought came to me, I could feel Becky's impenetrable gaze on me. Eve didn't know the dirty details. If I knew Becky at all, she likely hadn't even told Eve what a piece of shit her dad really was, and it was probably eating her alive that Rose and Eve were friends. But she couldn't tell her not to befriend the girl, she had no reason. Rose was amazing.

I moved to hug Eve, but this past year had changed so much, and I didn't feel as connected to her as I once did. We smiled at once another and she blushed a bit before going to sit beside her mother and baby brother. More people trickled in. The man that ran the grocery store for as long as I've been alive, neighbors that I vaguely recognized but had never spoken to, people in suits whom I assume were old coworkers of my dad. I had no expectations for how this day would go, but seeing the room slowly begin to fill up made me more emotional than I'd anticipated. Becky is situating her son, and I begin to walk over to introduce myself to him because a toddler is the least intimidating person in the room when Mickey walks in. I feel an instant flood of relief and pivot to shake his hand.

"Thank you for coming. I didn't realize so many people would show up."

Mickey shoves my hand away and wraps his long, gangly arms around me. Jen stands next him, sympathies twisting her expression as she rubs my arm and offers her apologies for our family's loss. Everyone has to say that it's the traditional thing you do when a loved one dies. You bring flowers, casseroles, and express sympathies for your "family's loss". But there were so many other things I could list that destroyed our family and they came long before my dad's cancer.

"Where's Josh?" Mickey asked. I try not to appear confused as to why he used his name and not Roach. Also, I mentally note that although so much has happened, it was all in the span of less than twelve hours. Mickey wouldn't know the truth about Rose, and he definitely wouldn't have heard about what happened at the pier and how I forbid Roach from showing his face today. I don't even consider telling Mickey and Jen the truth. In a few hours, I will close this chapter for good and be back in New York. If anything, it's helping me to realize that I might benefit from seeing a therapist to work through it all. Being alone seemed like the right thing, but I don't want to be alone when I die. I don't want my only legacy to be a box of pictures of my past and have nothing in the present to carry me.

I shrugged and turned toward Becky who is greeting the pastor that will be speaking to the room before we move to the graveyard. Eve pats the empty seat beside her, and there's something inside me that is relieved to have someone not think I'm the asshole. I don't know if we both accepted the shift in the dynamic at the same time, or maybe it was a bizarre comfort in such a strange time, death can bring

241

people together or tear them apart. But, I wouldn't be surprised if we never spoke or saw each other again.

Ben and Wesley held hands against the judgmental stares from some of the people in the room. Jen and Mickey appeared so connected and in love as they leaned into one another, their fingers woven together. Becky is slightly bouncing her son in her lap and Eve rubs his tiny hand with her thumb. Nobody in the room is crying, other than Ben. Even Becky keeps her usual stoic expression, likely to unravel in privacy. She's old school in that way.

The pastor begins to speak, touching on the finer moments of my dad's existence, which were few. We were all left with just as little as we always had, and I don't know why that surprised me. I felt a little disappointed that there was nothing new to learn, that he hadn't done anything noteworthy aside from pacifying my mother and settling into a lackluster career that gave him no drive or purpose. Maybe I'm being too hard on him, cruel even, but I struggle to believe he was happy with his life.

Half an hour later, everyone exited the Blue Room in hushed whispers and made the walk to the grave that was marked with a single tombstone with my father's name on it. I glanced at Ben over the casket and saw that he had pulled shades over his eyes. I wanted to ask why it was a single grave, but I didn't need to. Even in death my mother didn't plan to share space with him. Did she ever even love him?

More words were spoken about life and death and what comes next, and while the pastor drolled on, I felt a prickling sensation at the back of my neck. Something warned me not to turn, not to take my eyes off the casket, that this is the last I will see of my father and it's important to focus on that. But it's like an itch I needed to scratch, so I pulled my eyes away just for a moment and there she was.

There *they* were standing off a short distance away.

And I saw red.

John

Once again, that familiar pounding in my ears. The noise of the guests ran together like the teacher's voice on Charlie Brown. I couldn't make out the kind words nor well wishes for when Ben and I leave. My face grew hot with the embarrassment I'd felt that I couldn't control my reaction to seeing not only my mother, but the audacity of the two of them together. How long had it been going on that he would feel so bold? Did he think it would be okay now since my dad was dead and Ben and I were going away? Is that why he'd been so generous? I swallowed against the bile in my throat, the nausea in my gut that threatened to purge the breakfast I'd eaten. I smiled through the internal rage, patting arms and shaking hands, hugging Mickey and Jen while my eyes burned so hot I thought they might melt inside my skull.

Thunder roiled above us despite the clear skies. I looked to my left and saw the dark clouds pushing toward us, how fitting. "Ignore them," Eve's voice broke through the growling in my head. I didn't know how she knew what seeing them was making me feel, but I assume it was written all over my face. Or maybe, the town knew more than I thought, and my mother's return was obviously going to make me uncomfortable. Ben looked totally unbothered as he stood with Wesley, chatting it up with the man from the

244

grocery store. I blinked and attempted to calm myself, but I was so angry. No, I was enraged. I was fuming and betrayed. I wanted to strangle Roach. I wanted my mother to leave like she always did when we wanted her instead of staying when we didn't.

Becky clasped a firm but gentle hand on my elbow, "Do you want us to drive you home?"

"I can take him. I think Ben will be here a while, and it's on my way to work," Eve offered. Becky gave her a once over then looked to me to be sure that I was okay and understanding that I definitely wasn't, but her son was beginning to cry and squirm.

"Eve can drive me to the airport," I affirmed. My flight was not for another several hours, but I would rather sit in the crowded noise of the terminal than here for another second.

Becky nodded and gave me once last long squeeze. I wish I had savored it, remembered the smell of her and the way her aging body clung to me like a true mother's does. I don't even know what my own mother's embrace felt like, it had been so long since she'd held me in any capacity. I could feel them still hovering around like a disease, like hyenas waiting to pounce. If Roach thought for once second that he would use this day to force me into forgiving him, he could think again.

"Let's go," Eve said, tugging on my arm. "Say bye to Ben."

My skin tingled and felt clammy under my suit jacket. I was suffocating, but I didn't want my mother to see she'd rattled me. That would be her goal. It fed that demon inside her to know she made people uncomfortable. I don't remember walking to meet my brother. I don't remember a lot from the rest of that morning. It came in flashes over the years, little pieces I'd stashed away until I could complete the picture and truly understand what happened.

I remember hugging him even though I could tell he was still upset with me, or annoyed, or abandoned, whatever it was that we weren't going to talk about. The crowd thinned and the rain began to fall. Rose guided me to her car. We didn't speak, but we were walking fast. I remember the sound of her shoes on the grass, then when they hit the pavement.

Clack. Clack. Clack.

She kept trying to calm me, but the more she spoke, the more my insides boiled and bubbled. I just wanted to get in the car and go. I wanted to leave. I wanted to be back in New York where it was changing seasons and where you could buy big, fat pretzels on the sidewalks. I felt like I was going crazy with the panic. I'd tried different things over the last year to keep them at bay, but being thrust back into what caused them to begin with was completely overwhelming.

Eve rushed ahead and pulled at the passenger door, sensing my anxiety. The sky had opened, and the rain was falling in sheets. I could hardly see three feet in front of me. But before I could reach the car, there they were.

"Leaving so soon?" my mother's voice pierced my brain.

"Why did you come, Mom? Really? What did you stand to gain coming here?" I asked through gritted teeth. I didn't really want to hear her answer. She pulled a cigarette out and lit it, her umbrella tucked tightly underneath her arm.

246

"He was my husband, John. The father of my children. Of course, I was going to come and pay my respects," she said flicking her cigarette next to the ashtray but not in it.

"Not the father of all your children," I respond sarcastically, my breaths came quick and labored.

"No, not to all of my children. John, you need to get over that. It would have never been an issue if you hadn't been so self-absorbed as to leave us in the first place," she accuses. The panic is gripping me so tight that I ache all over my body.

"Come on, let's leave. It's pouring," Roach steps from behind her, his hand on her waist and I take a step, but Eve grabs my arm and pulls me back.

"Don't you dare blame me! You did this to our family! You left Dad long before I ever did. I had to move on! I had to get a life! I had to..." I was filled with pure, unadulterated hatred.

"You had to fuck your sister?" she interrupted raising her eyebrow and taking a drag on her cigarette. The rain and thunder were a symphony around us.

"Mom. I'm telling you right now. You need to stop. JUST STOP!" my hands begin to tremble, and I shove them in my pockets so she doesn't see.

"What, John? You're not mad at me. You're mad at yourself. Not only did you leave your dying father and your adolescent, helpless younger brother behind, but you took a perfectly nice young woman, and you ruined her. She had a good life before you came along and soiled it, like you do everything," she flicked her ashes towards my feet.

I clenched my teeth and force myself to say calmly, "I didn't do anything with her... and I didn't leave Dad, he told me to go. He said..." the nausea is too much. My stomach is doing flips as the guilt came flooding in.

"Oh, but you wanted to. You still do," My mom interrupted again and chuckled.

"Mom, I said stop," I turned toward the car.

"I talked to Ruth. I called them to see how Rose had recovered. Of course, she didn't want to say much considering I was the woman she'd stolen a child from, but she eventually coughed it up. I guess once you've lost someone you love, there's no need to hold grudges," she shrugged and took another drag as if we were talking about where to grab lunch after this.

"Lost? What are you talking about?" I am trembling. I hated her games and I hated how she knew exactly how to get under my skin.

"Oh? I figured Roach or Mickey would have told you. Rose went home, all in a tizzy last night after our conversation. She couldn't believe everyone had lied to her all this time. I agree, so trashy the whole thing. Anyway, apparently, she couldn't bear the thought of how disgusting you two had been and did it. She went to a Texas cakewalk," she began to giggle more as she threw her head back with her eyes wild as she fixed them on me.

"She went where? What the fuck are you saying Mom!" I had reached my limit. I was completely drenched; every drop of rain made my body feel more pressed to the ground. I couldn't move my legs and my heart rate was beating so rapidly I was afraid I might faint.

248

"She hanged herself, John. She got an extension cord from their garage and went to that beautiful oak tree in their field and... well you get the picture."

I blanked. I don't remember reacting to what my mother said or how I felt once she said it. All I know is I could feel something pop like when you have a good stretch first thing in the morning. I felt a second pop and it was oddly satisfying, relaxing even. Her arms were flailing around trying to push me off and untangle my fingers from her neck. I hear people screaming for me to stop, to let go. A smile slides across my face as hers fades. I couldn't stop squeezing. My hands grew tighter and tighter and as her body fell limp, I hear Roach.

"John! Don't!" I look to my right, and I see his face twisted and screaming in horror.

"John, what are you doing? Let her go!" I look back down and see my mother's lifeless body dangling from my hands. I drop her and watch her legs give way under her petite frame. Her arms spread in opposite directions across the concrete and her hair flutters around her like a thick golden halo saturated in a puddle of rainwater. Her neck is splotched with red and purple where my fingers dug into her skin. For the first time in her life, she looked peaceful. It was too late when Roach shoved me away coward that he was. It was too late. She was gone. My mother was dead and all I could do was smile, then laugh. I began to laugh hysterically. I was doubled over convulsing until I couldn't catch my breath.

John
Present

Suddenly, I feel a hand touch my shoulder and I'm falling, slowly sliding back into my body. Everything is still and I'm lying back on a couch I don't recognize.

"This time it lasted much longer, John. I think we've made a breakthrough here," he says as he offers me a glass of water and two small pills. I fumbled in my seat and looked at his outstretched hand confused.

"It's okay, John. It's normal to feel disoriented after something like this. Go ahead, take these. They will help you to relax," Marshall says, gesturing to the pills.

"What's happened? Marshall... where's Victoria?" I ask, anxiously.

"John, we've gone over this. Victoria does not need to be here during our sessions. She only comes to bring your meals and medication... you know this," Marshall writes something on his note pad.

"I... I don't understand. We live here. I feel so confused. Did I talk to my mom?" I glance around the room and notice bars on the window and diplomas written to 'Dr. Marshall Applebaum'.

"This is my office, John. You are a patient at Manhattan Psychiatric Hospital. I am Dr. Marshall Applebaum and you have been under my care for some time now. Victoria is one of my nurses who help care for you daily. You did talk to your mother, but not in the way that we are speaking now. We have just reached the point in which you were able to confront some issues that we have been working on for years." I blink as I stare at the doctor... *my* doctor sitting across from me. The pills begin to kick in and I feel my muscles loosen and the fog in my mind begins to clear. I fall back into the chair and the cushion gives under my weight. Flashes of my past click through my head like one of those children's toys where you pull the lever and another picture pops in. I remember. I remember everything.

I couldn't take it anymore. She had gone too far. She had pushed too hard, and I couldn't hold myself back any longer. My body was not my own as I leaped forward and gripped her neck so tightly that my hands cramped. I felt her windpipe crack within seconds. I felt tears and sweat roll down my face, mixing with the rain on my drenched shirt as I heard a wild sobbing.

Shut up. I'd growl glaring her in the eyes. But I realized, there was no way she could be sobbing. She was dead. It was me. I remember jerking sideways as Roach pushed me off her and I looked down at her body. I was completely detached.

"I'm sorry...I had to do it. I had to do it," I repeated this over and over. My sobs turned to giggles as Roach screamed for Ben and Mickey. I collapsed to the floor next to her body, laughing uncontrollably.

I must have looked insane, a just assumption at that. Mickey and Ben stood over my mother and me looking defeated. I don't know when Mickey had showed up. What had I done? I couldn't even make eye contact with my brother who was heaving as if he'd been running. I knew what I'd done would cause more pain and anguish for him than anything either of my parents ever did. I saw someone in the parking lot watching us and then race inside. Evidently, they had called 9-1-1 because within minutes, ambulance and police screeched into view. Mickey and Roach tried to help me to stand but my legs wouldn't hold me. The officers lifted me into the car and the EMS workers carried my mother on a stretcher into the back of the ambulance. The officers were so angry with me which was hurtful because they had to have known what a burden that woman was on everyone she encountered. On the ride to the station, I began panicking again. With each block, I was becoming more anxious and restless.

"Sit still kid," the officer commanded. He must have just been a couple of years older than me. I didn't recognize him. Was he from here? Was he married? My mind pondered this man's existence while my body writhed in my seat. I couldn't obey his command. By the time we reached the station, I had completely lost it. Within the hour, I was declared unfit to hold there and was placed under psychiatric care with Dr. Applebaum. He kept me out of prison by reason of insanity and the judge eventually had mercy on me and my *years of emotional neglect*. I was to stay under Marshall's care until rehabilitated. What does that even mean? It's not like I'm addicted to pain pills or alcohol. I'm stressed, that's it. Do I need help? Sure, we all do at one point or another, but how do you measure ones' mental wellness when it comes to something like this?

I have been able to receive phone calls. I had been a ward for over a year before Ben finally reached out. I didn't blame him. I was still so in and out of reality that it made no difference if he called every day or once a year. I wouldn't know the difference. Dr. Applebaum eventually diagnosed me with Post Traumatic Stress Disorder stemming from years of neglect from my mother. He also said that I suffer from an extreme stress and anxiety disorder. In one of our sessions, he mentioned my mother probably had issues of her own but was never properly diagnosed. Bottom line, I come from a history of crazies. Marshall said that had I not had this encounter with my mom, I may have gone much longer without an incident. There were too many events that I had never gotten help with that led to my blow up and unfortunately it ended in an 'extreme overreaction to an emotion I did not have the tools to handle'. I've been here for eight years. I've spoken to Roach and Mickey a handful of times, but I'm not sure if I was in my right mind when we spoke, so I can't guarantee whether they know about my condition or not.

I'm essentially alone. I've fabricated a life that I wish I had to cope with my loneliness. I had everything going for me before I got the call from Ben that dad had passed. I had suffered tragedy and overcome it but just couldn't deal with my mother. She was the one trigger that I couldn't push through and here I am. I sit here with no college degree, no career, no girlfriend, no penthouse, and no lovely in-laws who we have dinner with once a week. Somehow, right now, sitting here and soaking in my sad existence, I wished to go back into my false world. What was wrong with allowing me to believe that I was happy?

"John, do you have any questions?" Marshall asks me.

"I feel like I've been awakened from a dream to see that my life is no better than when I was a child. It's worse honestly. How am I supposed to get well and move on with my life if I keep doing this back and forth?" I ask, already knowing the answer but hoping he says something else.

"Well, that's what we are trying to work on here. There is no way to ensure that you will ever be well enough to leave. We have been trying different medications to see which are best for you, but they all have their side effects. The first year you lived in a strait jacket. Then we switched and you were doing very well for almost two years, then you tried to commit suicide. We moved to another and that's when the alternate world began. You've never really given up the want for normalcy, but we also haven't quite managed to get you to a place where you can mindfully live with what you've done. I have not given up on you John." His words were comforting but disheartening all at once.

I've failed him somehow. I've failed myself. I'm one of his more difficult patients, and he can't figure me out. I can see it in his face, but he's too kind to admit that I'm a lost cause. I guess sometimes we must recognize our limitations and find ways to work around them. If I've created this false life, then I don't see why I can't work to make it real. I was on my way there before; I could do it again. I know it's a long shot but what else is there? Once you hit rock bottom, where else can you go but up?

AIMEE PINARD

Roach

I pay for him to have the best care possible. It's the least I can do after what he's gone through. I check on him regularly. Sometimes he knows where he is and what he's done, but more often than not, we talk about Victoria and how they're living together and getting engaged soon. I cry every time we have those calls. John tried so hard not to become his parents, but here he is. It's mind blowing to see one person's entire life be filled with so much pain and sorrow. I never told Mickey about Rose, not that it mattered once he watched John murder his own mother with his bare hands. We both feel an obligation to him. We like to think if this were one of us, he'd do the same. Although maybe not. John was so angry at me in the end. Raged blinded him, but I guess if I'd seen my best friend with my mom like that, I'd be pretty pissed too. But Patrice was dealing with her own shit, too. She had to come back to a town that treated her like dirt, to a friend that hated her, a dead husband...she needed someone. I wanted to talk to him about it, eventually. I wanted to wait for the right time. Now, it doesn't look like I will ever get the chance, but he doesn't seem to remember my part in all this.

It was bizarre to see her lying on the ground like a rag doll tossed on the floor. Her eyes bloodshot from being strangled. Her beautiful, long neck positioned in an

255

unnatural way. I remember kissing that neck. Feeling her skin goosebump under my lips. That seemed so long ago. Like it happened in another universe. Her hair was knotted around her head. I shivered with want to smooth it back, make her look nice before anyone else saw her. She deserved better, the woman I loved. Looking down at her I felt a great sadness, not for myself but for her. I don't think anyone had ever seen the deepest parts of Patrice like I had. I don't even think Rick knew her that intimately. She could have been so much more than this, but because of her unwillingness to help herself, she's been reduced to a chalk outline on the sidewalk of a funeral home. In that moment, staring down at her body, I imagined my life had I gone off with her. Would she have left me anyway? Would this be me instead? Would I have still straightened my life out? Everyone has choices to make in life. I'm a firm believer that everything is connected and that each small decision that you make is a part of a much bigger picture that is revealed to you as you grow and mature. Here was one of my much larger and more profound moments. I feel lucky.

I try not to ever return to our hometown anymore. It brings back too many memories that I don't want to relive. I don't go back to my family's lakehouse either. If I have learned anything from John, it's to avoid all situations where negativity exists. As if returning to a place where something bad happened would only cause more bad things to happen. Whether it exists in our minds or not, I know it to be true. The human mind is a powerful thing. Even when it is held by weak people. Maybe even especially.

I have the local florist tend to Patrice's gravesite. Only half of her ashes were buried, I carry the rest with me in a porcelain vase and scatter a little in every new country or city I visit. I offered them to Ben, but he refused. He thought I would find more interesting things to do with it than he would. I like to think that traveling with me would make her happy and that wherever she is, she's looking down and smiling at all the places we are visiting together. Even the most broken people deserve to be respected and acknowledged. I pay for Rick's gravesite to be maintained as well. The half of her ashes that were buried lay side by side with him, which I'm sure he would have wanted, even though she didn't. The stone remains with only his information, but I created a smaller marker for hers, just for me. Maybe in Rick's version of heaven, they found each other again, and in the forms that best fit one another. They would live out their days as happy as he hoped they'd have been in life. There are so many unknowns about death and the afterlife. It brings me more comfort to think that when we die, we become ultimately healed. Nobody is sad, nobody is sick, and nobody is lost.

I'm afraid, however that this is the only way John will ever find peace. That's the main reason I can't talk to him too often and why I haven't had the balls to go visit. I can't look at him and see what could have very easily been me. I can't look at a person who I considered my brother and know he's gone. I deal with that guilt every single day, but I have faith that one day, he will come out of this. I just hope that when he does, he will be able to move on with his life without the fear that this will happen again. I've learned a lot from him or maybe I make different choices than I used to because of what happened to him. I don't think I'll ever get married. I don't want anyone to have control over my emotions and actions. It's best that people learn to keep a safe distance from others because you never know what's going on in that woman's head who sits next to you on the bus or the man who takes your ticket at the movie theater. Everyone has a story and I make it a point to pay attention and never make the same mistake twice.

Ben

It's always obvious when John and his doctor have a breakthrough. I get a call from him where he sounds like he's run a marathon and is riding the high of just crossing the finish line. There is always a drop, unfortunately. Our call starts off like anyone would hope.

"Ben! I can't begin to apologize for what I've done, but I want you to know that I've been able to get through some tough stuff with Dr. Applebaum today. He is optimistic that this could be it! I want you to come down and visit me in person. I want you to see how I've changed and improved." John always sounds so confident with his rehabilitation.

"I'm very happy to hear this, John. When do you think you can receive guests?" I ask.

"Oh, anytime Ben! You just come anytime, and I'll put my work aside for you." He is so energetic that it nauseates me.

"John...have you taken your meds today?" I am wary as I feel the conversation bending. He especially begins to fall off when he's tired and if he's had a breakthrough, I can imagine he's extremely worn out.

"Of course, Ben. I'm telling you, I'm better!" he sounds annoyed with me. I know I should be happy for my brother, but all of the patience I once had, has dried up. He sounds like our mother. Desperate yet hopeful but completely out of his mind. I knew the next words out of his mouth would be...

"And come hungry Ben. Victoria will make a roast! She makes the best roasts. Bring Tom, he will love it!" And there he goes. Right back down the rabbit hole.

I take a long sip from my whiskey glass and allow it to burn down my throat and calm my nerves. I've given up trying to get Roach to move him to another hospital. I know I'm the one who has the power to make that decision, but Roach is the one doling out the money for it, and he's John's best friend. I feel an obligation to consider his opinion. Wesley wants me to move him and be done with it, but I just don't have the money and John doesn't have the insurance, so we are stuck. He hasn't had a visitor once. Not once. He doesn't even notice which is even more pathetic than the fact that we have not shown up. Then again would *he* have come? John has been failed so many times in his life and by the people he cared about most. He never even talks about how angry he was with Mom. He can't talk about her at all without getting anxious. I've spoken to Dr. Applebaum several times, and he insists familiar faces would encourage his mind to move forward and I keep promising him I will come. But if he can't even get my brother to stop playing make believe with his nurse, then how in the hell am I supposed to have confidence that he can fix me? I don't believe in the whole rehabilitation bullshit. Everyone is screwed up. We all have our own shit. John just couldn't handle his like the rest of us. They've tried everything and he's stuck in his own world, and honestly, it's probably better than the real one anyway.

I'll go see him one day. I have tried many times, but I just can never force myself to go through those gates. I'm not ready to open that chapter and I'm not ready to forgive my brother for murdering our mother. As sick as she was, she didn't deserve what he did to her. He ended her life and shit on my father's grave at the same time. I can't let that go. I don't care how crazy he is. Mom was nuts, but he had a hell of a lot more than she ever did. We all have choices, and he made his. Now he must live with it. I used to look up to him, my own personal Superman. I never understood Mom's bitterness towards him all the time and felt like I needed to protect him the best way I knew how. As I grew up and my eyes were opened to more things, I started to see it all differently. John wasn't really a hero, he was coward. He ran away from home when it got too tough. He ran away from school, and then he ran away from Dad. All of that running got him exactly what he deserved. I'll go see him one day...when I can look him in the eye and not want to spit in his face.

AIMEE PINARD

Rose

It took a while for me to move past what happened
that summer. Not only had I been in this traumatic accident
and survived, but I also learned that I was adopted and that
the guy I thought I was falling for was actually my half-
brother. It still creeps me out to even think of it. I've never
told anyone, and after what happened...I still get chills
thinking about it.

I returned home after Patrice confronted us at the
pier to my mother wringing her hands at the door. I wasn't
late, but that was her way. My body vibrated with a mixture
of rage and the thrill of having experienced first-hand how
dark and disturbed Patrice was. I can see why John was so
closed off, why he never wanted anyone around her. But
there was a part of me that felt intensely intrigued, and not
because she was my biological mother, I felt no more
connected to her than some random stranger on the city
bus, but she was genuinely insane. Watching someone walk
that tightrope between sanity and insanity...I'd never even
seen a movie that disturbing.

The whole drive home, I'd rehearsed just how I
planned to confront my parents, my mother specifically.
How they could go my entire life lying to me, how they
sheltered me so obscenely that I almost hooked up with my
half-brother, or how my true parents lived minutes away and

262

I was never told. It felt dirty and wrong, but when I looked at my mother, worrying through the screen of my front door, I couldn't do it. I couldn't break her heart. I also couldn't open the opportunity for her to guilt me into staying here. So, I kissed her cheek and went to my bedroom, calling over my shoulder how I loved her and would see her bright and early.

I slept fitfully and thinking back, maybe it was my own body trying to tell me something because we were woken by a loud pounding on our front door. We had a doorbell, but either she didn't ring it, or we hadn't heard it. My parents emerged from their bedroom, bleary-eyed and disheveled.

"Who in the world would be knocking this early? Surely, not those Jahovas Witnesses again!" my mother spat as she roughly tied her robe around her waist and stormed toward the door.

When she pulled it open, my stomach dropped to my feet, and I was glad I hadn't eaten yet otherwise it might have come right back up.

"Yes?" my mother spoke when Patrice stood, still in the same clothes as last night.

"I was wondering if I might speak with Rose?" Patrice stood nervously fidgeting on our front porch. I saw no car behind her. Had she walked? How did she even know where we lived?

"Absolutely, not," my mother stepped protectively in the small opening of the door. "You shouldn't be here, anyway and I suggest you move along."

"I just wanted to...I wanted to apologize for how I behaved. Sometimes I can be a bit impulsive," her voice shook, but I couldn't see her anymore now that my mother was acting as a human shield. My father placed his hands on my shoulder, lightly tugging me into the kitchen, but I planted my feet firmly on the ground.

"Well, that's all well and good, but it isn't my daughter's job to absolve you. Time to grow up, Patrice," she said before closing the door. I watched as she took a heavy intake of breath and blew it out before turning to face us. "Okay, then! Let's all get freshened up and I'll make us a lovely spread!" Breakfast was my mother's favorite meal of the day. She always made far too much food and ended up bringing the leftover to the church to serve the hungry, or the volunteers who showed up to do odd jobs around the grounds.

I waited until my parents had closed and locked their bedroom door, a habit since I was very young and prone to walking in without knocking. I raced out the front door, hoping Patrice hadn't gotten far, but as expected, she was on foot.

"Why did you come here?" I called out after her.

Her body froze and I was able to really grasp the entirety of her in the strangest of ways. She was a slight woman, thin and delicate, but her expression held an otherworldly knowing, as if she knew everyone's secrets without being told a single word. When she was fully facing me, her eyes were wild but focused, if that can even be a thing. I felt as though the were holding me in place so firmly that it was like a physical touch.

"I wanted a chance to see you," her voice was just above a whisper.

"You already saw me. Why are you here?" I pressed.

"I always wanted a daughter," she began, her shoulders relaxed, and her eyes finally broke from piercing into me and skittered around our property. "Rick only gave me sons. I would have been better if I had a girl. If I had you. But he took you away, it wasn't my fault."

I crossed my arms over my chest, "Who is my father?" I didn't want to give her any comforting words. The little John had shared, it was clear she wasn't just a bad mother to him and his brother, but actively so.

"His name is Ted. He's a lovely man. I saw he could make a daughter, so I just...well, I wanted what Becky had. I wanted a girl," she smiled, but tears fell from her eyes as she stepped closer to me. "And Rick was so selfish, he--"

"Stop right there," I held out a hand, "Rick died, so please don't think you'll get any sympathy from me over a man who can't defend himself. I have parents, lovely parents who provided for me. Seems to me, I was much better off without you. Please leave." I said before turning on my heel and hurrying back before my parents realized I'd gone out.

"Don't let yourself get stuck here like I did!" she called after me, but I didn't respond. I didn't so much as offer her a wave because what I did with my life would not be tainted by her. I hoped as much for John as well.

When I heard about her tragic accident, the first thing I wanted to do was call John, but the number to his home was disconnected, and Eve told me that he was already on his way back to New York. All she said was that Patrice suffered a stroke or something at the funeral home, nobody seemed to have any other information. Now that I knew her husband was my father, a whole new basket of questions arose. I chose not to talk to Even about it, I doubt she was told, and I couldn't be the one to burst her bubble. I've come to terms with being adopted, that my parents did what they thought was right to protect me. I didn't really know Ted, and now I can understand why. I'll never know how much Becky knew or at what time, but if it were me, I guess I'd do anything to protect my child too. Even if it meant lying to them.

I hate even admitting that I feel relieved for John, he's free now. He'll be able to live his own life for once without the fear of her popping up and ruining it. Ben took off and I think he's happy to disconnect from everyone and everything. Caring for a dying parent can really mess you up, and I worry about him. I got his number from the internet, so I could try and reach out, but he didn't seem as interested in getting to know me and I don't know if after all this time, he's even interested in having a relationship with me.

I've been at school for several months now, and I keep thinking about making a drive to Times Square, check out Central Park, see if by happenstance I can run into John and, in a sense, start over. We are different people know, and it would be nice to have a sibling, as strange as that may sound. Maybe I'll look him up soon. Everyone needs someone to lean on from time to time, otherwise we all fall down.

ACKNOWLEDGEMENTS

I began writing this book as an assignment for a scriptwriting class in college. It was my senior year, and I had only just realized how much I loved storytelling. It was too late to change my major, and it felt "too late" to figure out how being a writer would translate in my adult life. So, it was shelved. Fast-forward a little over seven years, a move, a marriage and two babies later, my husband encouraged me to get back to writing. He dug up my old hard drive and found the pages I'd completed for that class. I turned it into a little novella and have been writing ever since!

I thank Chris often for allowing me the time and space to do the things I love to do while raising our girls. Being a stay-at-home mom is not often seen as "real work", but he values my role in our home as well as the idea of having things that are just for me and not wrapped up in being a wife and mother. But what he doesn't realize, is that those two titles are why I find joy in writing, being a wife and mother inspires me constantly.

Thank you to my amazing community for being invested in this process and supporting me while I took the time to figure out how to proceed with my stories. Thank you to my mother-in-law's book club for hosting me and being genuinely wonderful company. You are profoundly interesting and lovely women and I deeply appreciate you all.

This story, in particular, was written, published, unpublished and re-written, and to my family and friends who have read all versions, some of you multiple times, you are the real ones. Thank you. Thank you. Thank you!

AIMEE PINARD

About the Author

Aimee Pinard is a Houston, TX native and when she is not writing, you can find her curled up with a book, riding her bike on the local trails or chasing after her three daughters— one of which is much furrier and has four legs. She loves her monthly bunco and book club, but very much a homebody with her husband and their shared love of a glass of wine (or whiskey) and a good series. With her youngest being diagnosed with Type 1 Diabetes, she is an advocate for the JDRF and is committed to raising awareness while connecting with other T1D families. Visit her website for updates on what's to come!
www.aimeepinard.com

Instagram : @_aimeepinard_

Printed in Dunstable, United Kingdom